Crush

ADDICTED TO YOU
BOOK ONE

LYDIA MICHAELS

Dedication

To that guy. You know who you are. Your determination guided our muse and your success proved love can prevail in reality as much as romance novels. The "days of dust, which we have known" are gone, and the wait was worth all that is today.

Listen to the Addicted to You Playlist!
Click Here to Listen!

Prologue

December

HER HUSBAND SAGGED ALONGSIDE HER, his skin damp from their exertions, heart beating in sync with her pounding pulse. "My beautiful December."

Austin's gaze held hers as she came down, his chest pressing slowly to hers as his teeth gently closed over that oh-so-sensitive place on her shoulder, nipping before soothing away the sting with a slow slide of his tongue. Even hard on the heels of a mind-blowing orgasm, December shivered with need from his touch.

She sighed, body limp with contented exhaustion. "That's one way to celebrate our anniversary."

"That's just round one." His warm breath whispered against her temple as he gathered her close. "Don't even think of getting away from me."

She blinked into his stare, encompassed by his whisky brown eyes. "Never." Wrapping her fingers tightly around his forearm, she nestled into his strength.

His gaze softened, his familiar eyes creating a sense of home that lived deep in her heart. "Do you know what it does to me when you look at me like that, like I'm your hero?"

She couldn't answer, weighed down by a cacophony of emotions so gratifying they tempted irrational fears that nothing could remain this perfect forever.

She gently cupped his jaw. "You *are* my hero, Austin Garret." Her dominant man who usually read her needs before she could identify them herself.

Unabashed—and why should he be—a cocky glint flashed in his eyes as his chest rumbled with deep, male satisfaction. "Mine. You're all mine, Mrs. Garret."

Being that he took such thorough care of her, his arrogance was amusing. Charmed and honored to earn his claim, she fed his ego. "All yours."

"Will you love me as much on our fiftieth anniversary?" he whispered, his body so close she could count the gold flecks in his eyes.

"Of course not," she teased. "I'll love you more."

The bedding rustled as his grip tightened, possessive yet gentle. Her body pressed softly into the quilt she hand-stitched, each little thread chosen with the love and care she held for this man and their home. Her mind settled in the limpid shadows of contentment.

Home. It wasn't much, but it was theirs. She never believed a person could ever be this happy, this full of gratitude for such an ordinary, traditional life.

"What are you thinking?" He stroked her hair, his work-roughened fingers slipping through the dark strands with a whisper of sound.

She smiled and stretched within the protective circle of his arms. "That I love our home. I'm not talking about our house, but our actual *home*."

"You make it a home, Ember, *you*."

Despite being the most capable and confident man she knew, she loved his perception of them as completing one another, that he might somehow be half a person without her. She felt the same. "You're my home."

They rested together, breath and thoughts mingling, lost in serenity until gravel crunched in the distance and the sound of a big motor brought them back to reality. Served them right for falling into bed the moment Austin got home from work.

Holding up a finger she shut her eyes and gestured at the precise moment a horn blared. So predictable. So Cord. Austin let out an exasperated sigh and she choked on a giggle. Their friend always had impeccable timing.

"For fuck's sake," Austin grumbled, affection and tolerance hidden in his tone as he eased his arms away from her and sat up.

"You told him to come for dinner." Studying his perfect ass as he stepped into his jeans, she was in no rush to find her clothes.

"I also told him it was our anniversary."

Sitting up, she pulled the sheet to her chest. "Don't even. He said he didn't want to intrude and you told him we were celebrating this *weekend*. He turned you down three times. You were very insistent."

Caught, he rolled his eyes and shook his head. Dropping his elbows to the mattress, he kissed her. "If we don't feed him he eats out of cans."

"I see through all your grunting and growling, Mr. Garret. You're just a big softy behind all that muscle."

He pinched her hip and she yipped.

Rising, he picked up his wrinkled t-shirt and shoved his arms through the sleeves. "I'll let the asshole in. Take your time, but don't leave us hanging too long. Cord ain't as pretty to look at as you." He paused at the door, his gaze roving over her bare shoulders and naked form hidden by the quilt. "Thank you for another beautiful year of marriage."

Heat rushed to her face as her lips pursed in a smirk. "You're most welcome, sir."

"How did I ever convince you to marry me?"

She snorted. "Convince me? You straight up told me." Her voice deepened, mimicking his, "You're gonna be my wife one day. You'll see." It had been thrilling, and she'd responded immediately to his dominant approach.

His brow arched. "Do you have any regrets?"

"Not a single one. Now go take care of our friend before he rethinks our invitation. I'll be down in a couple of minutes."

One

December

TWO YEARS LATER...

Cool air nipped December's face. The rest of her body remained tucked under a thick layer of blankets and every part of her demanded she stay in bed. But if she didn't get up, things wouldn't get done and there was plenty to do, especially since the boiler didn't seem to be working.

With a shiver, she braced her body against the chill and shed the covers. Her toes immediately sought refuge in her fluffy slippers as she rolled out of bed and shuffled to the bathroom.

Eyes still blurry with sleep, her sluggish mind came awake as the wintry chill bit at her ankles, assuring her the furnace absolutely wasn't working. Another concern to add to the building list of catastrophes.

Frigid water spit from the tap and she quickly washed up. Returning to the bedroom, her gaze snagged on the large bed, one side of the comforter creased and slept under, the other half undisturbed.

The ache that set up camp in her chest ten months ago hadn't subsided. Her body merely adapted to its hollow presence and tolerated the pain a little better each day. True loneliness was an agony she once assumed only death could bring, but she was wrong. Her husband was still breathing, still living, but present only in a half-life of his own making.

Sighing, she dragged another layer of clothing over her head and bundled up for the day. "Just a ghost passing through," she mumbled, as she wandered down the steps.

Coffee. She needed coffee. Her slippered feet swiped over the carpet, as she chafed her hands and squinted at the thermostat. Sixty-eight. Definitely not accurate. Chafing her hands, she breathed warmth between her palms, needing every bit of heat she could find.

Living in the Endless Mountain region of

Pennsylvania wasn't always pleasant, especially in January. The cost of oil was killing them and they were in the red with all three fuel companies. It would be a miracle if she finagled a delivery today—her charm was wearing thin.

Snatching the threadbare throw off the bench by the front door, she folded it into a shawl and entered the cold kitchen. Setting the coffee to brew, the scent of dark roast filled the air as the tempo of percolating drops broke the silence. Knowing Austin was still sleeping, she quietly set to unloading the dishwasher and tidying up the kitchen.

A tiny kernel of bitterness, buried deep in her psyche, formed an additional tough, thin layer. Every empty beer can she found tightened the vise clamped around her heart. Austin wasn't an alcoholic—she didn't think—but he liked his beer. Liked it a whole lot lately. Liked it enough to spend thirty dollars on a case rather than on their accumulating debt.

She didn't relish another fight, but they had to confront the fuel issue together. Finding her husband on the couch, she frowned at the mess surrounding him.

Oh, the hours an insomniac could sleep. Austin was hardly enjoying a well-deserved rest, so why did she care about disturbing him? She thrust the thought away, dispatching it to where the other disloyal wifely thoughts hid, the accumulating pile becoming somewhat disturbing.

"Austin." She nudged his shoulder. "Austin, wake up."

He grumbled and rolled to his side, burying his large body in the cushions of the couch and blindly reaching for the quilt that twisted around his hips. "Fucking freezing in here."

"I know. We're out of fuel again."

He groaned and pulled the quilt over his shoulders. "You call?"

There would be no *calling*. Getting a delivery with an outstanding balance the size of theirs would take a face-to-face encounter. "They won't come if we call. One of us needs to go there in person."

"Jesus." He sat up and scrubbed his palms over his face, groaning and obviously irritated to have his sleep interrupted. "Give me the phone."

"Austin, they won't talk to you. You have to go there."

"That's bullshit. Just give me the phone."

She passed her cell over and waited as he dialed, straightening the mess on the coffee table as he attempted to place an order. There was no pleasure in being right, but when they denied him and he ended the call her point was proven.

"Fucking assholes," he muttered, tossing her phone onto the table.

"I'll just go down there and see what I can do."

His laughter came out as a scoff. Somehow the blame for their financial crisis always seemed to fall on her shoulders as manager of their not-so-significant wealth, though she *never* blamed him for losing his job.

"Why bother?" he snapped, curling back under the blankets.

She blinked at him as he abandoned the problem and left it to her to find a solution. "Maybe if we both go..."

"I'm not begging. Fuck them. We'll find a new fuel company."

But they'd already been through all the local companies. Didn't he get that? Swallowing her frustration, she returned to the kitchen. A lump formed in her throat, crushing her windpipe, but she swallowed back the urge to cry and bicker. Arguing was pointless.

The coffee pot hissed and chugged as the last few drops leveled in the carafe. December swapped out her slippers for thick hunting socks and boots before filling her favorite travel mug.

Layering up in a hat, scarf, and her warmest coat, she glanced at the sleeping form curled on the couch and sighed. Grabbing her keys and gloves, she made a beeline for her old Cherokee.

Her body clenched with shock the second the cold leather seat penetrated her jeans. The starter groaned and frosty air tunneled through the vents as she gave the wipers a few minutes to work the newly fallen snow off the windshield. She should use the ice scraper, but it was too damn cold.

Blurred shades of green, sprinkled with snow dotted the wavering horizon. When she first saw where Austin lived, she'd fallen in love. Endless mountains with tiny, picturesque towns tucked into hidden valleys. It had been springtime of course, followed by a radiant Indian summer, and breathtaking autumn. By the time her first winter in the Endless Mountains came around, it was too late to go back.

She loved where they lived, except during winter. The early months of the bitter cold represented endless seclusion, short days, and multiplying dollar signs, especially of late.

Her parents should have named her June or September. Any warmer month would have been more appropriate since she despised the intrusion of cold weather that came hand in hand with December. Better she'd been born a grizzly. Hibernating sounded much wiser than trekking out in this nasty season, but if she ever wanted to get warm she needed to take care of some things.

She let the snowy divots guide her wheels, giving the Jeep slack as she backed out of the driveway and puttered toward Willow Street. Her mind wandered to Austin. How long would he sleep today? He was usually up before noon, but he'd been pushing that envelope more and more each day.

She didn't want to get her hopes up. If she expected anything out of the ordinary or even remotely close to what they'd once shared, she'd only wind up crying herself to sleep in their empty bed. Who was she kidding? It was *her* bed and her bed alone. He hadn't slept there in months.

Tarnished memories contrasted with her husband of late, sliding painfully into a once perfect image like shards that were too sharp and would never stop needling. Meeting him and Cord had been a pivotal moment in her life. The precise attraction to Austin's tall, handsome persona anchored her almost instantly. The confidence he oozed attracted her the most, though.

She'd known intuitively Austin would take care of her and live up to his promise of being the head of their household. While his offer of safety and security called to her with a role she'd always craved, it was his romantic side, intriguingly mixed with spine tingling dominance, which sealed the deal and married him to her heart long before they ever exchanged a single promise or vow.

Despite their recent troubles, he was such a capable man, the good times still outweighed the bad. Her drive passed in a scattered trip down memory lane. So many ordinary days molded into extraordinary moments since meeting him. He had always been the most thoughtful person she knew, until recently.

As memories ricocheted through her mind, she could almost feel Austin's strong fingers entwining with hers, his once exuberant energy pulsing between them.

"I have a surprise for you. Shut your eyes."

It had been one of many ordinary days that his thoughtfulness had surprised her. Trusting him to guide her safely, she lowered her lashes and clung to his hand as he led her through their house, a smile playing on her lips. "What is it?"

"You'll love it." And she had no doubt. Sometimes Austin knew her better than she knew herself.

He positioned her shoulders and stepped back. "Open."

It was silly to get so excited about a turned bed of soil, but it had been something she'd dreamed of for a long time. As she stared at the small victory garden lined with herbs and peppers, her smile bloomed.

"A garden!" She spun and kissed him, his arms already open and waiting to catch her.

"Do you like it?"

"I love it! It's exactly what I wanted. Thank you."

He took her hand again, pride and satisfaction radiating from his hold. "Over here you have potatoes. And these are your tomatoes. I put in some rhododendrons along the edges to keep the rabbits away."

He'd been so proud of that garden, not because it took a lot of work, but because he delivered something he knew she wanted, something she could manage that would make her happy. Days like that played so vibrantly in her mind she could almost feel the heat of the sun and sense the warmth of his tireless affection.

But of late, she woke up in a marriage she no longer recognized. Where was her best friend? The keeper of her secrets—and her heart? Where was the man who led? She loved Austin, would always love him, but perhaps he no longer loved her. How else would he have let them fall so far?

When he'd first swept her off her feet he actually had her convinced the romance would never end. But now that man had vanished and a stranger took his place.

At what point does a woman admit her marriage is over?

She shoved the gut-wrenching question away, where it landed on the accumulating pile of other things she couldn't bear to face.

"We're just in a rut," she muttered, as she cranked the wheel and pulled into an empty parking space. Thinking the worst was a defeatist's attitude and she wasn't a quitter.

But it was the same useless excuse she'd been feeding herself for ten months. It had to be a rut. Ruts were temporary, patchable. Eventually, Austin would come back to her, return to the man he'd been before losing his job.

Her gloved fingers tightened on the steering wheel. The car was just starting to warm, the heat of the cab seducing her away from the unsavory task ahead. Her gaze followed a bundled figure unlocking the door of K&G Heating. Great. It was Mrs. Gibson. That woman could be so condescending. December shut her eyes and dropped her forehead to the backs of her knuckles still hugging the wheel.

"Please." It was a prayer sent to anyone merciful enough to hear it. Her pride had withered to levels below begging long ago. Begging was better than freezing.

Once the interior lights of K&G kicked on, she drew in a deep, cleansing breath and removed her keys. The tinkling bell above the door mocked her tentative entrance. Mrs. Gibson's smile turned to a scowl as December removed her hat and her identifying dark hair tumbled down.

"Ms. Garret." The woman knew she was married, yet insisted on addressing December with a patronizing *Mizz* every time she visited the office.

Flies with honey.

December smiled, her cheeks burning from the chapping cold. "Good morning, Mrs. Gibson. How are you today?"

The older woman's brow puckered as her lips pursed with insincerity. "Fine. Are you here to make a payment?"

Words caught in her throat as she forced a quivering smile. "Actually, I was hoping to order a delivery."

The woman laughed, brittle and without humor. Her gaze darted to the florescent pink Post-It on the desk. Yes, their balance had obtained Post-It status. "You owe eight hundred, forty-two dollars and three cents."

Was the three cents really necessary? "I'm aware, and we should be getting some money to you soon. But right now it's thirteen degrees and we're out of fuel."

"I'm sorry, but without a payment I won't be able to schedule a delivery. You haven't put anything toward your balance since before the New Year."

God, she hated this woman. The mention of New Year's reminded her of the miserable Christmas they hadn't celebrated. They would eventually pay off their bill, but without work... one couldn't draw blood from a stone.

Marshaling her thoughts, her smile trembled. "I know. I'm sorry about that. It's been tight. Surely, we can work something out."

"I'm afraid not."

Lips pressed tightly as she took in the older woman's resolve, December's shoulders tensed with the need to scream. It was freezing! Where was her compassion? Beady eyes, cold as coal still in the seam, stared back.

December pivoted and tacked her hat on her head. Choking back tears of frustration, she returned to her Jeep. She couldn't give up, so she drove to Mount Top Fuel.

The reception at Mount Top was much the same. Mr. Flemings printed their statement, illustrating their balance was in the six hundreds. That put them over a grand in debt and she still had one last fuel company to visit. Her heart sank as she accepted the day would be long, and in the end, still freezing. The icy road blurred as she blinked back threatening tears. What were they going to do?

Their unemployment had run out months ago and Austin hadn't been called for any interviews since last year. She'd gone to see about her old position at the bank, but the teller who'd taken her place had no intention of giving it back.

She should have never let Austin convince her to become a homemaker. How was she supposed to know this was where they'd be a year later? The bridge commission was a great job. They had a hefty savings, great benefits, and were ahead of their mortgage. Now, their benefits had lapsed, their savings had run dry, and they were a light sneeze away from losing their home.

Her stomach knotted as she combated the endless anxiety twisting her insides into some misshapen piece of origami. There was no use going to the next fuel company. Their balance was likely close to the eight hundreds there as well, pushing over two grand of debt in fuel alone. It wasn't worth the cost of gas to drive there only to be rejected.

Wiping her eyes on the back of her glove, she made a wide turn and headed for home. They'd figure it out. Austin would just have to chop more wood. It wasn't aged, and it wouldn't burn properly, but it would have to do.

An abrupt change in traction shuddered through the steering wheel to her clenched fingers. Tears distorted her vision as the Jeep pulled sideways, sliding on ice and stealing her control.

"Shit! Shit! Shit!"

The car spun, the landscape blurring in swirls of white and gray as she sucked in a breath and held it tight in her lungs. "Fuck!" A sharp cry ripped from her throat.

The vehicle seemed weightless for a split second as every muscle in her body tensed, preparing for the impact. She was going to die.

Flashes of her home, her husband, her cold morning and everyday routine whirled like a kaleidoscope in her mind, so vivid it overtook her vision for a suspended moment in time.

The Jeep slammed down, her body jostling roughly in the seat as her head smacked against the window. Pain lanced through her temple telling her she was still alive.

Shaking uncontrollably, she blinked at the snowy windshield, forcibly releasing her grip on the wheel. Everything hurt and she couldn't tell if she was in a ditch or completely flipped upside down.

She searched for her phone, but her purse

had spilled. Nausea overwhelmed her as she reached over the seat, and she forced a labored breath out hoping to balance her equilibrium.

Her vision wobbled as silence morphed into a sharp whistle and her body went limp, her voice too weak and her fingertips too far from the mobile device to call for help.

Two

December

DECEMBER RECOGNIZED the soft crackle of fire and the familiar scent of burning wood. Warm. She was so warm. Her toes curled in her wool socks as she snuggled deeper under the covers and sighed—

"You awake?"

On a gasp, she tensed and jolted upright. With a flash of light, pain vibrated down her spine and she winced. She hissed, pressing a hand over her eyes as discomfort settled over her entire body.

"Whoa. Easy there, kiddo. You've got quite a lump on your head."

If she opened her eyes too quickly, surely she'd vomit. She peeked through her fingers, getting a grip on her senses, and blinked through the soft glow of firelight. There was no mistaking the man sitting across from her.

"Cord?"

"To the rescue—*duhn-dun-nuh-nah!*"

She frowned at his strange little superhero jingle and glanced at his battered couch. He needed new furniture. "How did I get here?"

"Well, you slid off the road just before the covered bridge. Your tires are freaking bald. What the hell's Austin thinking letting you drive around like that?"

She slid off the road? "Where's my Jeep?"

Cord shrugged, his broad shoulders moving easily beneath the broken down fibers of his flannel shirt. Tiny creases framed his steel blue eyes and his dark curly hair was in its ordinary disarray. "I called Bernard. It's probably being towed out of the ditch or already at the shop. I told him to put new tires on for you."

"You what?" She bolted forward, and immediately regretted the action. Gripping her temples, she collapsed back to the couch. Her skull was throbbing.

"Maybe you have a concussion. I probably should've taken you to the hospital, but that would have taken another hour and you were freezing. I just wanted to get you someplace warm—fast. If you want to make the drive now that you're up, I'll take you."

Thank God he hadn't taken her to a doctor. They had no medical insurance. "No. No hospital. I'm okay." She wasn't. "I need to use your phone. I have to call Bernard and tell him to cancel the tires."

Cord scowled. Sometimes he responded so much like Austin. He'd been Austin's best friend since pre-school. It seemed only natural for them to share the same expressions and mannerisms.

"You can't drive that thing with bald tires, Ember. You're lucky you didn't get pulled over, or have a tire split in weather like this."

As right as he was, they simply couldn't afford four new tires. She didn't care if Cord knew they were broke, but Austin was very private about such things, even with his best friend. He could barely talk to her on the matter. The man had more pride than he could afford.

But Cord was right. If she'd known what shape the tires were in she would have borrowed Austin's truck. Her husband usually made sure her oil was changed and their vehicles were safe, especially since hers was over ten years old. The sting of realizing he'd neglected yet another need of hers knocked the breath from her lungs. It wasn't that she couldn't maintain her car on her own. It was the fact that Austin set out these roles, and every day she was hit with another letdown when he didn't live up to his own edicts.

Cord moved to the couch and gently rubbed her shoulder. "Hey, relax. You look like you're ready to cry. Are you in pain?"

If she cried it wouldn't be the result of her physical injuries. Her throat constricted as she struggled to breathe. Adrift and terrified, suffocating by the weight her alpha male had vowed to bear, her once manageable world seemed to be swallowing her whole. With the burden of her own responsibilities, and now his, the ever-increasing pressure on her shoulders threatened to break her once and for all.

Thoughts of Austin coming home in the not-so-recent past, bone weary, yet so proud of his ability to provide for them flew through her head.

"My sweet housewife," he'd tease as he tugged at her apron and stole a taste of the meal she'd plated. She missed the feeling of his arms wrapping around her. "Dinner smells great, but I bet you taste better."

She'd kept their home with equal pride, in a dated dynamic they both revered because it worked—until he lost his job.

With a shudder, she faced the present. Now he did nothing. No longer did she need to worry about being available to him, because he showed no interest in her, sexually or otherwise, not even in regard to her safety.

Something neglected and desolate snapped inside of her. Pressure built behind her eyes. The weight on her shoulders transcended to pressure in her chest. Unable to hold it all inside, she burst into tears.

"Hey, hey, hey, why are you crying? Shit." Cord stood, clearly uncomfortable with her show of emotion. "Is it your head?"

He paced, searching for something in the kitchen, clattering objects across the counter, and returning with a paper towel and his keys. "I'll take you to the clinic. Here, blow your nose. Stuff's dripping out."

She snagged the rough paper and blew. "I'm sorry," she sobbed. "It's just... He... The car... How many beer cans will I clean up tomorrow? It's so quiet all the time. Mrs. Gibson is a *bitch*! We have no fuel! The wood doesn't burn right, because we used up all our seasoned supply. My toes are always fucking numb! And now my tires are bald..." The last of her tirade came out in a wail.

As she blubbered, muttering half thoughts and nonsense an outsider wouldn't understand, she struggled to get her emotions under control. Reeling in her hiccups and sobs, she apologized for her outburst as Cord's face morphed into utter panic.

She wiped her sleeve under her nose and sniffled. She was tougher than this and it surely was not the time or the place for a breakdown.

When she focused on his expression again, a wet laugh squeaked out. Poor guy. His eyes were wide with horror. She sniffed and repeated her apology, "Sorry. I'm just a little overwhelmed."

Unblinking, he watched her cautiously. "Was that some sort of female exorcism? I didn't understand a word you said, but you should know that's my last napkin. After that, all I can offer you is a coffee filter."

She laughed again, despite the shard of agony it sent through her temple. That was Cord, the quintessential bachelor. Her paper towel was drenched with snot and tears. "Do you have any toilet paper?"

"Uh-uh. Coffee filters."

Scrunching her nose, she swallowed her revulsion. "You're wiping your ass with coffee filters? Cord, that's disgusting."

"It's not like I do it all the time. I just ran out. I was in a pinch." Glancing away, he muttered, "They're just ruffled, glorified tissue. It isn't like I'm brewing with them when I'm done."

She gagged, her stomach still queasy from

the knock she took to the head. "Please stop talking before I throw up."

He shrugged and shifted his feet. "I think I should take you to the clinic."

"Please, no. I'm fine. I just got upset." She wasn't fine, but she also wasn't paying for a doctor to tell her so.

"You want some soup then? The market had a ten-for-five on tomato, so I have about a hundred cans to get through. Well, ninety-seven."

She shook her head, still cradling her temple in her palm. "You bought a hundred cans of tomato soup?"

"It was a good sale. And I like it. Don't know how I'll feel once I reach the other end of fifty, but for now I'm enjoying it."

Suddenly the whole diet of nothing but tomato soup on the tails of the coffee filter conversation really was enough to make her puke. "Oh, God...there's something wrong with you."

"I'm thrifty," he stated proudly.

"Cord, you own one of the most successful hardware stores in the county and you're wiping your ass with coffee filters. There's thrifty, and then there's cheap. Don't you sell paper products at the store?"

"The coffee filters are a result of laziness and attention deficit. A pretty girl in the paper aisle distracted me."

She smiled. "I'll take some soup."

As odd as their conversation was, it was nice to converse with someone other than herself or a debt collector. Strange that Cord was Austin's best friend and he didn't have a clue how bad things were for them. He might enjoy a sale, but he was probably one of the most generous people she'd ever met.

She rested her eyes as he clattered around in the kitchen. The mere sense of someone else close by, up and functioning was a comfort.

Cord returned from the kitchen and handed her a mug of soup. The heat seeped through the ceramic and warmed her palms. For a fifty-cent meal it smelled wonderful. She grinned with appreciation. "Spoon?"

"I can't find one right now. Just sip it."

She smirked and pressed her lips to the mug. The thick liquid heated her belly and helped calm the nausea. She hummed with satisfaction. Who needed a spoon? Drinking soup had faster effects.

"Why aren't you at work?"

He sipped his own mug. "It's supposed to be my morning off."

"Sorry." Her tension slowly eased once her belly wasn't so hollow. "I should probably call Austin and let him know where I am." She glanced around for her purse. "Cord, where's my stuff?"

"Uhh...probably at Bernard's."

Shutting her eyes, she wilted into the couch. "Great."

"Sorry. I saw the Jeep and panicked. My mind was only on getting you warm and safe."

"It's okay. Please don't apologize."

"Do you want me to go get it?"

"No. I can get it later. It isn't like there's anything valuable to be stolen."

He frowned but made no comment as he reached in his pocket. "Here, use my phone."

She took the fancy device and tried to navigate her way to the actual phone function. "How do I use this?"

"Oh." He slid his thumb over the screen and handed it back to her. "It's ringing."

She stilled when she saw the screen. Instead of saying Austin's name it said *Fart Barfunkle*, and there was a picture of an elderly, wrinkled man in underwear. Holding it up so he could see, she asked, "Really?"

"Sorry. I'm a small child."

Shaking her head, she pressed the phone to her ear and waited for Austin to pick up. It eventually went to voicemail. "Hi, babe. It's me. I, uh, had an accident. I'm okay. Cord found me and I'm waiting at his house until I feel well enough to move. Call me when you get this. Oh, call Cord's phone, because mine's at the body shop. Love you. Bye."

"He'll probably be here to get you in a few minutes."

She stilled as Cord carried their mugs to the sink. Is that what he really thought? Did he actually have no idea the state his best friend was in? "Well, if he doesn't get the message, could you give me a ride home in a little bit?"

His broad shoulders twisted and he rolled his eyes. "Like that will happen."

She hesitated. "I just mean...if he's busy or something." *Or sleeping.*

"It's Saturday. What the hell's he got to be busy with? His wife was in an accident. He'll be here. And when he gets here I'm gonna give him hell about letting you drive on those shitty tires."

"About that." She laughed nervously. "Could you not say anything to Austin?"

Cord stilled, all natural humor leaving his expression. Even in her woozy state, she sensed the authority behind his usual, relaxed demeanor. "What the hell's going on, Ember?"

Upon agreeing to move to Austin's hometown, Ember knew she'd be leaving her friends and family behind. She'd inherited *his* friends, though most of them had made themselves scarce this last while. But Cord was her husband's *best* friend and embodied such confidence. Surely she could confide in him.

Letting out a long sigh, she slouched into the couch. "Things aren't good at home. They haven't been for a while."

He scowled and returned to the living room. "What do you mean?"

"He's been out of work for ten months. Austin's the kind of guy who needs to work."

"Has it been that long?" He shook his head then said, "He'll get back on his feet." The conviction in Cord's voice spoke of his love for Austin.

"I know he will," she quickly agreed. "But it's wearing on him."

"You mean financially? If you guys need any—"

"It's not just that."

"But money's part of it. Jesus. Why didn't he say something?"

"Because he's Austin. You know how he is."

"You mean stupidly stubborn? Yeah. I know how he can be." He returned to the kitchen and lifted the lid off a jar on the counter. When he returned he unfolded a wad of cash. "How much do you need?"

Panic grabbed hold of her. "Cord, I can't take your money!"

"Don't be an idiot, December. How much?"

There had to be well over a thousand dollars in his hands. The temptation to accept was so fierce her common sense fled. Without much conviction, she whispered, "I can't."

"December." A thread of dominance wove through his tone and something she'd thought buried stirred in response, sending a shiver up her spine.

Cord locked his stare with hers and continued, "You guys are my family. I should've realized, with Austin not working, you'd be struggling. I feel like an out of touch jerk. I'm gonna help you."

Her head hung as the pressure of their burdens threatened once more. "We're so fucked up, Cord."

He sat on the edge of the coffee table in front of her. In a soft voice he said, "Hey, life's hard. I should have offered sooner. I wasn't thinking how rough this would be with you no longer working at the bank."

Yes, and when she was a teller, they always managed through Austin's layoffs. She'd also seen Cord's deposits. His little hardware store brought in a *very* healthy income according to his deposits and savings. There was a chain store on the outskirts of town, but Cord's family had been local for several generations and the town folk preferred his hospitable service to the conglomerate competition. A couple grand to him would be a drop in the bucket, but to her and Austin, it would be a life raft they desperately needed.

"It's bad," she confided in a low whisper.

"Should I get a pen and paper?"

There was that confident male again. Cord sometimes came off as just a pokey, careless, backwoods guy, but December knew he was so much more. The man had a heart the size of Texas and would do anything for those he loved. He was also book-smart, which made up for what he lacked in common sense.

Once he found a notepad and a dull pencil, which he sharpened with a steak knife, they began making a list. "What about cable?"

She laughed. "Cable? What's that? We haven't had cable since June."

He didn't see the humor. "Do you owe them?"

She nodded. "Last I checked we owed a hundred and twenty, but they tack on a late fee every month it goes unpaid. The only thing we're caught up on is our phone bill. I can't let that payment lapse in case Austin gets a call for work."

By the time Cord had a full column of numbers, he blew out a slow breath, but never once gave the impression this was an unmanageable situation. "Okay, so I have the fuel companies, the electric, cable, water and sewer, the mortgage, and your late payment on Austin's truck repair. How about medical?"

"We have none."

"You don't have any medical? December, you were in a fucking car accident today! What if you needed x-rays or surgery?"

She shrugged. She was well aware of the risks. "I think I'll be okay." Seeing he was still pissed, she tried to pacify him. "We still have auto insurance."

"So you think insuring your car's more important than your health." He shook his head. "What the hell is Austin thinking?"

"He's not."

The two words fell between them with the impact of a brick shattering a pane of glass. Life was full of cracks, but when things really broke, they couldn't always be fixed.

Cord's sharp blue stare cut into her. "What's that supposed to mean?"

Her shoulder lifted in a half-shrug. She figured Cord would understand, seeing as he and Austin held a lot of the same values and thoughts on gender roles. It was no secret that her husband preferred to be the man of the house and she knew his friend concurred. No one ever expected Austin to stop manning up when life got tough.

"He's different. He's not the man I married. This isn't the life he promised me, not that I expect to be treated like some sort of princess or that he had any control over getting laid off, but he's the one who asked me to quit my job. He made all these promises I never expected. I'm okay with the fact that life got in the way of his plans, but he can't seem to accept defeat—or even a setback—and he refuses to ask for help. I'm sick of fighting about it."

"You guys are fighting?" He didn't raise an eyebrow or appear overly shocked, probably due to all the financial troubles she'd revealed, but there was still a hint of surprise in his voice.

"Not really. We sort of just ignore each other at this point."

His face twisted with disbelief. "But you're Austin and December. You guys never fight."

"Every couple fights, Cord."

He tossed the notepad aside. "I don't get this. Austin isn't a dumb guy."

"He's just in a rut." There was that broken record again. The small pile of disloyal thoughts shifted as though prodded to life by her denial.

"Well, he's being a fucking idiot. He's the head of the household and shouldn't forget it—

no matter what." He rubbed his hands roughly over his face.

Just like her husband, Cord had a way of always looking in need of a shave. Dark hair lined his strong jaw, which was set with tension. The more she explained what was going on with Austin the more irritated Cord became and the less he could disguise the intensity hiding beneath the surface of his casual lumberjack flannel and worn jeans.

He was so familiar. Cord represented a huge part of the life she'd adored and somehow another luxury they'd sacrificed over the past few months. How had that happened? She missed seeing him around their house.

"I miss having you over for dinner."

He laughed, the dry chuckle a near sarcastic snort, as her comment broke the tension. "You guys never ask anymore. I'm not going to invite myself over to play third wheel like I used to. But seeing that my best friend neglected to tell me how hard up he's been puts things into perspective."

Her hand pressed into the dark denim covering his knee. "Hey. Austin loves you. We both do. This isn't about you. It's about him and his stubborn pride."

"More like stupid pride. How are you guys even affording groceries?"

She smiled. "Well, now that I know about the tomato soup blowout at the market we'll be stocking up." She didn't think it necessary to mention the furniture she'd sold or the research she'd done on meals to make for under a few dollars. Nor did the weight she'd lost with her distaste for bologna and other cheap fixes seem significant. Maybe Austin wasn't the only one with pride.

His grin was forgiving and sweet. "There's no tomato soup left. Some guy cleared them out. You're gonna have to wait for the chicken noodle special."

"That'll work."

~

Their light hearted repartee lifted the mood a trifle and December gratefully sat back while Cord made a few calls and straightened out a few of their debts. She only agreed to accept his help if he agreed to keep a clear record of everything so they could eventually pay him back.

As he argued with Mrs. Gibson to get a delivery up the mountain to their house this late on a Saturday, she set to tidying up Cord's personal disaster. He was as much of a slob as Austin, but there was a familiar satisfaction in taking care of someone who appreciated her efforts and simple touches.

She wasn't shocked that Austin hadn't called, but she was surprised Cord hadn't mentioned it again. If he planned on being more involved in their situation, he'd eventually see for himself what she'd tried to explain.

She was washing the last of his dishes when he found her in the kitchen. "You should have fuel again shortly."

Shutting off the faucet, she faced him. "I can't thank you enough, Cord. You saved us."

He shook his head and placed his large palms on her shoulders, pulling her close for a companionable squeeze. Her body nearly collapsed at the show of affection and she melted against him. For so long she'd been starved for something as simple as a hug.

"That's what friends are for." His hand rubbed over her back as he balanced his chin on her head, but he didn't let her go. "Hey, you found my spoons!"

She laughed and stepped away. "Yup. But I had to throw away your small metal pot. I don't want to know what was glued to the bottom."

He made a sound like Snoopy in distress. "I don't want to know either. Sometimes I try to get creative when I watch the cooking network. It's better when I stick to canned soup."

She laughed. "You need a good woman to take care of you." His expression turned guarded and the energy of the room shifted. Had she said something wrong? "Sorry, I—"

"Don't apologize." His easy smile fell back in place. "You're right. But a good woman isn't always easy to find. *Which is why* Austin better get his shit together before another man snatches you up."

She smiled, but something about that statement left her unsettled. Everyone knew she wasn't going anywhere. She loved Austin. What they had was beyond special. He'd own her heart forever, which was why he'd eventually climb out of this rut. He had to. Otherwise, who would look after her soul?

Time for a change of subject. Putting the last dish in the cabinet, she carried two cups of coffee to the weathered kitchen table. "I have a proposition for you."

Cord arched a brow. "Oh? I love it when pretty women start a conversation like that."

"Settle down there, tiger. I was thinking, since the woman who took my job at the bank isn't giving it back—"

"What a wench."

"—maybe I could work for you...at your shop."

"You wanna work at the hardware store?" His surprised smile was priceless.

She shrugged. "I don't know a lot about tools, but I could help with the cashier stuff and maybe organize some of your inventory. I mean, you don't have to know what a tool is to hang it up on a display and make it look pretty."

"Tools aren't supposed to look pretty, Ember. They're supposed to look intimidating and phallic."

She laughed. "Phallic?"

"Sure. Long, hard, tapered tips, smooth yet solid, good for drilling, pounding, and the like." He grinned. "Men are obsessed with tools for a reason. It's a matter of masculine foreplay."

"Right... Well, what about the job?"

"It's yours."

"Really?" Her face split with a grin. "Just like that?"

"Sure. It's winter, so my summer help's away at college. I could use an extra set of hands. Plus, it'll be fun having you there. When do you want to start?"

"Tomorrow?"

"Perfect."

"You're a lifesaver, Cord."

He held up a finger. "I don't want to hear any shit from Austin about this though. If he gets mad, you tell him you asked before I offered."

"He can't afford to get mad. One of us has to work. He can't, because if he takes a side job outside of his local he'll lose his place on the call list —not that being on the list is helping. His phone hasn't rung."

Union pay was good, but the work unpredictable. And taking a side job meant getting bumped on the waitlist.

"There's always work, December. A man just has to come to terms with the position offered in order to meet certain goals and keep his promises."

Lowering her gaze, she whispered, "He's trying."

When Cord didn't immediately reply, she peeked through her lashes at him. His mouth was pressed into a thin line and his blue eyes were narrow slits. "No, he's not. He's hiding like a little coward. Sooner or later he'll wake up and smell the coffee and hopefully be able to fix all that he's neglected."

Hearing someone criticize her husband stung in a way that called up her blind loyalty, but Cord's words were undeniable. It was clear he'd lumped her into the "neglected" category, and his protectiveness on her behalf seemed warranted, though humiliating.

If it were anyone else criticizing her husband she'd have jumped to Austin's defense, but this wasn't just anyone. Cord knew Austin as well, if not better than his wife. He knew what a great guy her husband was, which made Austin's recent lack of effort all the more shocking.

On the ride home they were quiet, and it was a comfortable silence. But as they neared the base of the drive that led up the mountain to her home, she needed to say her piece.

"Cord?"

"Yeah."

"Thank you for your help. It means the world to me. I promise I'll pay it all back."

"No worries. Even if you hand it to me when we're old and senile and I can't remember what it's for, I know you'll square up. You're a good girl, Ember. You can always count on me."

"I hope it doesn't take that long."

"Makes no difference. I know you guys will get back on your feet sooner or later and all of this stress and worry will be water under the bridge."

Her chest tightened with the weight of her gratitude. "Thank you."

Keeping his eyes on the road, he reached over and patted her knee. "That's what friends are for."

When they pulled in front of her house, the

easy energy in the truck shifted to something dark and heavy. Glancing from the dark house, where only the blue light from the television glowed in the window, and back to Cord's face, her stomach twisted. She gathered her scarf and gloves.

Cord's jaw tensed under the shadow of his stubble and his eyes narrowed. Her husband's disinterest reflected in every telling sign of neglect surrounding the house. His truck wore a week's worth of snow and the walk hadn't been blown out, but haphazardly shoveled—evidence that she'd cleared the most recent dusting, not Austin.

As she suspected, Austin was completely ignorant of her day's challenges. She'd be willing to bet he hadn't even checked his voicemail. Her shame hardened into additional resentment, and having her humiliating situation exposed to Cord stung more than any column of debt ever could.

She jumped out of the truck, lacking the energy to make another excuse on her husband's behalf. "Thanks again."

His brow tensed, but he kept further comments of their situation to himself. "I'll pick you up tomorrow morning at seven-thirty. Your tires should be done by the end of the day."

Nodding, she quickly shut the door and hustled inside.

The television muttered the mindless chatter of some dated DVD from their collection. Austin was awake but didn't rise to greet her. His head pressed to the armrest and his stare glued to the set. A can of beer dangled from one hand.

"Where you been?"

December stilled, her fingers caught on the last button of her coat as her jaw locked. Where *had* she been? Never in her life could she imagine coming home after a nightmare day saturated with shame to a husband who sounded more put out by her absence than concerned by it.

Her emotions roiled, fighting to the surface, but exhaustion dulled her ferocity. Knowing tomorrow would be a much-needed step in the right direction, she reserved the last of her strength for something that would actually help. No good would come out of having another argument with a man who couldn't face the magnitude of their problems.

Yanking off her hat, voice calm, she answered, "Out."

"We're out of cereal."

She tossed her gloves on the bench along with her hat. He didn't deserve an explanation.

Fuck his cereal. After several deep breaths she said, "I'll add it to the grocery list."

Finding his disinterested presence unbearable, she pivoted and went up the stairs to bed. Her bedtime was getting earlier and earlier with each passing day. She used to stay up until midnight. Now, there was no reason to be awake after five. There was no point in waking early either, at least not lately. But tomorrow would be different.

She laid out her clothes for the next day and showered. The fuel had been delivered and heated water was deeply appreciated, not that Austin had even remarked on it.

Braiding her damp waves out of her face she tied it off. Though her hair had always been long, their financial setbacks put getting a trim on the farthest back burner. What usually reached the middle of her back now fell to her hips. She draped a towel over her pillow and shut out the lights.

Staring into the dark, her mind wandered between unpracticed prayers and worries. *Please bring my husband back to me. I don't know who this man is, but he isn't the person I married.*

A tear rolled from her eye to her temple. The sound of him shuffling around in the kitchen carried through the house. Cabinets snapped shut, conveying his irritation with the empty shelves, and undeserved guilt smothered her. *He* could stock the pantry if he wanted something. But she couldn't figure out what he wanted anymore. He used to want her.

It was like he no longer saw her, just looked right through her, when she used to be all he could see in the whole world. No matter what she did, he stayed away—alone—wandering through the house at night and sleeping all day. She had pride too, and he'd been chipping away at it, scarring her with deep tattoos of doubt.

Something happened to a woman when her husband no longer touched her, when he didn't take charge and exert his will to meet her needs, and reassure her. First there were the superficial frustrations of unrequited desire, but then it became something worse. The insecurity, fear, and uncertainty ate away at her insides.

Her self-esteem fractured, perhaps beyond repair. Tiny little shards of self-worth were all she had left. Even if he came to her now, begging and full of apologies, she feared someone might get cut.

This rut seemed to get deeper and darker every day. She was losing sight of the light and worried she'd never see herself out. She needed to feel alive, feel something. She needed to reclaim control and pull herself back to her feet, which was why this job with Cord was imperative.

The tender spot on her scalp served as a painful reminder of the past several hours. She'd take it though, because no pain no gain, and her life had taken an upward turn today. She had to take back the control she'd so willingly surrendered if she ever expected them to recover.

Three

December

SHE HAD BEEN awake for hours, full of nervous energy and excited optimism. It had been so long since she felt anything close to hope and she welcomed the pleasant mood. Eager to escape the house and Austin's sodden presence, she'd busied herself salting the steps and even swept the snow off Austin's truck—hoping it might provoke him to go somewhere and do something while she was gone. She'd been back inside pacing for the past twenty minutes awaiting Cord's arrival.

The horn barely had a chance to honk before she was out the door. After taking the steps carefully, she rushed to Cord's truck and climbed inside.

"Howdy, little dwarf."

Biting off her mitten, she clicked the seatbelt into place. "Dwarf?"

"Yeah, you know...whistle while we work and all that. We're off to work."

"Are we heading to the coal mines? Those dwarves were miners."

He backed down the drive with practiced ease. "Whatever. There's coffee for you in the cup holder."

"Wow. It's been a while since someone thought to make me coffee. I hope you used a fresh filter."

"I should have never told you that."

"I'm not judging." She paused. "No. That's a lie. I'm totally judging. In fact, I brought you a present." Reaching into the deep pocket of her parka, she withdrew a roll of toilet paper. "Tadah!"

He laughed. "Well, aren't you sweet? My ass thanks you."

It was such a refreshing experience to enjoy easy conversation, as familiar as riding a bike. Having someone to chat with made her realize how much she missed such commonplace things.

Rather than dwell on the negative, December sipped her coffee, ignoring the fact that she was over her two-cup limit and would be a hyper maniac in an hour.

"Was the heat working when you got home?"

"Yes! I took the longest, hottest shower of my life. They made the delivery while I was still at your place. Thanks again."

"Ember, stop thanking me. It's no problem."

"I can't help it. I don't know what we would've done without you."

He was quiet for a moment, his focus on the road. "Did you tell Austin?"

Her mind went to the reception she'd had last night. It didn't matter if Cord was asking about the loan or the job, the answer was the same. "No."

"Is this something you plan on keeping from him? Because I'm not sure I'm comfortable with that."

"He knows we have no money, or he should. He has to understand we've accumulated debt. What difference does it make if we're indebted to you or mean old Mrs. Gibson down at the fuel company?"

"That woman is something awful, but still. It makes a difference."

"How so?"

"Because Austin will most likely have issues with me knowing about his circumstances."

Frustration had her words lashing out before she could draw them back. "Well, they're my circumstances too, damn it."

"Easy, kiddo. I'm just saying you should probably tell him I offered to help you guys out for a while."

"It's not a while. I'm working now. I'll pay you back and as soon as Austin returns to work everything will be back to normal."

"Why are you afraid to tell him?" There was protectiveness in his tone and December hurried to offer reassurance.

"I'm not afraid of Austin. I just don't see the point in having another fight. It's done. You already cleared everything up and now our debt is to you instead of bill collectors. If he's not going to lift a finger finding a solution then he's just going to have to deal with the solutions *I* choose."

It sounded like a fine plan and she chose not to see any duplicity in it. Austin brought this crashing down on himself the moment he gave up honoring his half of their 'partnership'.

"Drink your coffee. You're moody in the morning."

"I'm not moody. I'm... Sorry. I shouldn't snap at you when all you've done is help. Sometimes I feel like a tea kettle without a steam valve, about to explode."

"You need to get laid."

She froze for a moment. There was no teasing in his tone, only matter of fact certainty. She scoffed at his very nearly accurate inference. She needed intimacy...physically and emotionally speaking. "You have no idea."

He glanced at her, blue eyes inscrutable, then frowned and returned his focus to the road. Silence reigned, and when they reached the store she was drowning in guilt. She shouldn't have jumped down his throat. Cord was right. She needed to tell Austin about the loan, but when was she supposed to do that with him sleeping all the time?

Or drunk.

He was concerned about cereal. Fucking cereal! Meanwhile, she was juggling fuel companies, getting in car accidents, dealing with the remnants of what she was pretty sure was a concussion, and trying to figure out a budget for their next meal.

Her plate was full. He'd made no concessions in his little self-pity parade to comfort her, so why should she go out of her way to inform him of the measures she'd taken to manage the things he'd neglected?

There was the pain. His greatest oversight

wasn't their finances or the upkeep to their home. It was *her*—his wife.

God, why did the continuing reminders of his neglect stab her deeper every day? She should be used to it by now. But her wounded pride never got a chance to heal, because every morning dawned with the reminder that her husband was on the couch *again*, her needs forgotten.

"Hello? December? We're here. This is the part where you go in and make the big bucks."

Shaking off her depressing thoughts, she forced a smile. "Sorry. I zoned out. Right. Big bucks. Let's get to it."

Noting the signs of worry in his furrowed brow, she preceded Cord into the shop. It smelled of sawdust and house paint. The unique scent agreed with her. The high, unfinished ceilings left the wide-open aisles cool, down to the polished cement floor.

"Put your stuff behind the register. I'll give you a tour before we open."

Her purse was still in her Jeep at the body shop so she didn't have much. She wedged her hat and mittens into the sleeve of her parka and stashed it behind the counter.

"Here, put this on."

She unfolded the red apron emblazoned with *Bay Hardware* and slipped her head through the loop. For some reason it made her smile. Tying the laces at her back, she faced him.

"I'm ready to work."

He grinned. "Red looks good on you."

The temperature dropped as they passed through the sliding doors and entered an outdoor area with two heat lamps just starting to warm.

"This is our garden section. It's fuller in the summer months when we stock plants and such, but we still keep it open in the winter to house the overflow. If anyone's looking for larger equipment like lawn mowers, grills, or fire pits, this is where you'd direct them. Shovels and salts are out here too, but we also keep a supply by the register. If you think we're running low, let me know. You won't be able to haul the fifty pound bags on your own."

"Are you calling me a weakling?"

"No, I'm implying I'm a gentleman and offering to do the heavy lifting for you."

"So sweet," she teased. And something she'd come to expect of men like Cord—and Austin. With a pang, she pushed the observation away.

He led her to the first aisle where the scent of fresh cut wood was strongest. Towering stacks of lumber loomed far overhead and a sort of lift thing was parked at the end of the corridor.

"Aisle one is lumber. We do some general

cutting if customers need it. Any questions about lumber, just page me, and I'll handle it."

"Do I get to drive the...forklift?"

"No."

"You're no fun."

"Next is plumbing. Sinks, vanities, toilet seats, washers, and such are here. What? Why are you laughing?"

"Cordovan Charles Bay, there is a huge display of toilet paper in this aisle. Shame on you!"

He shrugged. "I'm forgetful."

Shaking her head she followed him to aisle three. He gave her a quick rundown of each department, electrical, auto, heating and cooling. "This is the paint section. Eventually I'll show you how to mix, but for now just page me when a customer has questions."

He walked her down the tool aisle and described various things that looked sharp and scary.

"Is there an inventory of all this stuff in case a customer asks where something is?"

"Under the register I keep a big, black binder of inventory. Everything's alphabetized in the front and cross-referenced with an aisle number. We just got new computers so if you type in the SKU a picture will come up and it'll tell you if we have it in stock. If not, we can always order more."

"Okay. Good."

"And if it's something that's not in our inventory, we can order it anyway. I usually ask for a twenty-five percent deposit and the customer has ninety days after it's delivered to pick it up."

"I never knew you were so organized. What's your excuse for your house?"

"This is different. My business is my livelihood. I can't dick around if I want to compete with the monopolies."

He was so serious. There was that totally different side to the man she'd watched make an ass out of himself more times than she could count. It was sort of intimidating and alluring, authoritative and capable all at once. Austin used to be that way...

Shoving her thoughts aside again, she followed Cord to the home goods aisle. She was familiar with this part of the store and needed little explanation. When they'd purchased their house this was where they found their carpets, light fixtures, and hardware.

"I'd like you to get familiar with the stock catalogues back here," he said, as he directed her attention to the little table in front of the mock kitchen. "We don't have the space for the kitchen displays the bigger stores do, but we can provide everything they offer if the buyer's willing to wait a few days for the shipment. Because we don't stock every popular item, we save on overhead and can usually compete with the prices of the bigger guys. Problem is, because we don't have an in-your-face display, people usually assume we don't offer as much in that department."

He grabbed a big binder and handed it to her. "You can start with this one. Keep it at the register and look through it. Once you're familiar enough with the stock, trade it for another."

"You want me to sell kitchens?"

He shrugged. "You love to cook. You look good in a kitchen. I think you could sell the shit out of mine if you knew what we offered."

His praise—no matter how caveman—hit her in places too long neglected. She smiled and held the book close to her ribcage. "Thanks. I'll do my best."

Nodding he led her to the back. "Here are the public restrooms, water fountains, and customer service desk. I'm usually wandering around or in the front, so we hardly use this area, but it's there all the same. The regulars know they're better off getting service at the front."

"Why don't you use the customer service desk?"

He shrugged. "Man power. It's usually just me. When the college kids are here over the summer I stick one of them on duty, but this is more of a hands on setup. People have questions, they know to find a red apron and ask.”

He continued moving and she stood in place, blinking as she processed his words. If Cord was understaffed or open to hire help, why hadn’t Austin asked for a job here? Austin could have gone to him for a loan and Cord would’ve given them anything they needed. Ah, right. They were freezing and suffering and her husband’s stupid *pride* was only making things worse.

Sure, she could memorize inventory and talk up the kitchen sinks and work a register, but she was useless when it came to cutting wood or hauling heavier items. Austin would be great working here. Was it the pay? She hadn’t discussed a salary with Cord, but knew it would be lower than union pay. And maybe Austin had misplaced loyalty to the union that forgot he existed.

Scampering after Cord’s retreating back, she turned into a small room that smelled of coffee. He gestured. “This is the lunch room. There’s a fridge over there, a microwave, and some paper products in the cabinets. I usually just grab lunch from somewhere in town, but you’re welcome to use whatever you need.”

“Cord?”

"Yeah?" he turned, sucking in his lower lip as he usually did when his mind wandered. Funny how she stored those familiar details about him in the back of her mind.

She had to confirm her assumption. "How come you never offered Austin a job here?"

He blinked, appearing confused. "I...did."

"You did? When?"

"The day he got laid off and about every time I saw him after that."

Outrage boiled anew. Austin never mentioned Cord offering him a job. "Why didn't he take it?"

"I don't know. I can't match the pension and benefits he was getting working for the bridge, but I could've come close to his hourly. I guess he always expected to be called back to work sooner or later. Believe me, after learning how much you guys were struggling, I want to strangle him too." He shook his head. "I don't know what he was thinking letting things get so out of hand."

"Bills stress him out. I've always managed the money. He's been so moody lately and down on himself, I haven't really explained just how bad things are."

She was minimizing, still protecting Austin long after he stopped protecting her, but it was habit, like a smoker reaching for a cigarette even when they knew it wasn't good for them. *Or an alcoholic reaching for a bottle...*

"A man should know, or at least have some vague idea what his financial situation is, especially a man like Austin. You don't tell your woman to quit her job and ask her to be a stay-at-home wife when you can't take care of her."

While an outsider might find his phrasing dated, she accepted it. Cord and her husband were made up of the same fabric of values. She'd found such a dynamic encouraged old habits like chivalry and attentiveness. The way Austin and Cord believed couples should live—the way she and her husband *had* lived—made her feel cherished and cared for, making all of these shifts that much harder to stomach.

Austin had truly convinced her such a mindset could work, but perhaps there was an explanation as to why lots of couples weren't out there living like 1950's sitcoms anymore. Another excuse rolled off her tongue.

"Maybe that's why people stopped living that way. It takes two incomes to run a home nowadays."

There had to be a reason such dynamics were almost obsolete. Perhaps it was practicality over preference. She couldn't be the only woman in her twenties who longed to take care of her man and be taken care of in such a passé fashion. Could she?

Cord shook his head. "It doesn't require a fortune for a man to occupy the role of head of the household, Ember, although it absolutely takes resolve and motivation. Trust me, I watched my father manage it through many hard years. It's a big responsibility and not one that can be shirked when things get rough. Besides, a man needs to work. Why do you think my dad still takes the weekend shifts here? It's all part of the role and it never ends."

His words showcased her greatest fear, hitting her like a punch. "Maybe *I'm* not motivating him anymore," she practically wheezed.

"Bullshit. This has to do with him, not you. Don't let his crap make you second-guess your value. You're a good girl, a good wife, and he's a fucking idiot for making you doubt that for even one second."

Good girl... The term struck a chord deep within her and she shivered before focusing on the rest of his words. He sounded so absolute and she desperately wanted to believe him. Except, the two people who should be defending Austin were suddenly questioning his ability to live up to his principles and fulfill his promises.

But why undermine Cord's assertion? He was right. Cord was a lifeline and she grasped his offer of help with both hands. Despite the difficulties ahead, Austin being the biggest, there was no place to go but up. She preferred to face such obstacles with her husband at her side, but that didn't mean she couldn't stand on her own if needed.

Reaching out, she squeezed Cord's arm through his flannel shirt. "Thank you."

He gave a curt nod, one big hand covering hers with a reassuring pat. "It's about time to open. Why don't you take that book up to the front and I'll meet you at the register? We can get started on familiarizing you with the catalogue and the register."

"Sounds good." Her voice was small, tight with emotion.

She hadn't realized how abandoned she'd been feeling until Cord reminded her what having an alliance felt like. Loyalty wasn't a word she was examining too closely at the moment.

Four

Cord

CORD'S MOLARS locked as he watched December make her way to the front of the store. Her small figure seemed diminished, somehow, a far cry from the happy woman he'd come to know...and love. What the fuck was going on with Austin? His fist closed over his phone, the case creaking, as he drew in a calming breath.

Austin had always been a prideful motherfucker, but this was beyond bullshit. They'd been friends since they were in diapers. December was a great girl and his friend's neglect was simply unacceptable.

Sure, he'd been a little put out when

Austin had set his sights on her, but she'd never come between them. He hadn't lost a best friend when Ember came along. He'd gained one.

He didn't like to think about the distance that developed between them over the past months. They'd stopped inviting him over to their house and he'd interpreted that as a need for space. Maybe the distance pricked a little, but he honored it. Now, he cursed inwardly at the truth of the matter. They'd needed him and he hadn't known. And being a friend meant he'd always have their back—both of them.

In the past two days he'd seen and heard enough to question everything he knew about the man he trusted more than anyone else in this world. Why? What the hell would make Austin change when he'd been the same predictable guy all his life? What happened behind closed doors might be none of his business, but seeing Ember break yesterday crossed a line.

He hated when girls cried. Fucking hated it. Girls wept, he got that. But December sitting on his couch crying about Austin's fuckup was not cool. It wasn't her fault. This all pointed directly back to Austin.

The man had *everything*. Sure, he got laid off. Shit happened. The economy was in the crapper and Austin's type of work came with no guarantee. But there was no excuse for this sort of ignorance.

December was a fucking mess because of Austin. Her cheeks were sunken in and without their normal rosy glow. Her eyes were puffy and red with little purple moons beneath them, marring her pale skin. Too much worry and not enough sleep. And he didn't even want to get into how thin she'd gotten, something he'd noticed when she'd tied her Bay's apron, the sash cinching around her *twice*. And when he'd hugged her yesterday, he noticed the sharp angle of her shoulders.

Austin's number one priority should have been making sure she was taking care of herself —as her husband he should have insisted on it.

But Cord felt just as responsible and guilty. If he hadn't backed off, thinking they needed their own space, he wouldn't have missed all the red flags. Why did he pull back at all?

You know why...

He shoved that voice into the recesses of his brain and focused on the immediate issues. He and Austin had always been of the same mindset when it came to women. They both wanted to be the providers, the decision makers in the relationship. However, that dynamic didn't work when one made stupid, dumbass decisions.

He punched out a text.

. . .

> Call me, you fuck. We need to talk. Enough of ignoring my texts and messages.

Shoving his phone back in his pocket—not expecting a response—he headed toward the front doors to open for the day. Chances were, he wouldn't get a reply, but that didn't mean he'd stop trying.

He was involved now. Something had to get through to Austin. If December couldn't, then maybe a swift punch to the face would work. He'd give Austin until Friday to contact him, and then he was hunting the motherfucker down.

December was perched on the stool behind the counter, her nose wedged in the inventory book and the kitchen supply binder open to her left. "Hey, kiddo, how you making out?"

"You have everything really organized. I should find my way in no time."

December was a smart cookie and he had no doubt she'd do fine here. He was serious about her pushing the kitchen sales. She had a sort of charisma that sucked people in. He wanted that magnetism working for him and liked the fact that rediscovering a small level of her independence might restore a bit of the spark in her eyes.

Sliding behind the counter he got a whiff of her hair. It was fruity with a trace of something feminine. Totally December. "Here comes your first customer."

She perked up. "Good morning, Mr. Winchester."

Her greeting came naturally, and grumpy old Mr. Winchester stilled, a smile replacing his usual grimace. Huh. Cord never knew the old fart had teeth.

"December," the man hummed, as he pivoted and moseyed toward the counter, his bowed legs filling out his worn Levi's. "What are you doing here?"

"This is my new job. Can I help you find something today?"

Everyone in town knew December from her time at the bank. "I'm looking for a piece of hardware to match this old latch."

Eyes enchanting, she smirked as if she and the old man shared a secret, her charm stealing the remainder of his focus. "What are you working on this week?"

Cord frowned. How well did she know the old coot? What was he working on *this week*?

Mr. Winchester took some weight off as he

leaned on the counter and grinned at the help. "Found an old chest of drawers I'm planning on sprucing up and surprising the missus with. She saw something similar on one of them home shows a while back. I'm sanding it down and refinishing the wood in a nice cherry."

She turned the man's pudgy hand over and drew his attention to a smear of finish. "That looks like a pretty color."

The old geezer chuckled and flushed. "Maybe I should pick up some soap while I'm at it."

She grinned and patted his weathered knuckles affectionately. Dear God, it was like watching a snake charmer seduce an old crotchety python.

She collected the small latch he'd brought with him. "I think we have something similar to this. It's over in hardware. I'll walk with you."

Mr. Winchester raised a wiry brow. "Well, Cordovan, it looks like you finally made a good decision in the company you keep."

"We aim to please," he replied, surprised he could even form the words, as the odd couple strolled off into hardware.

A while later they returned with a shopping cart full of everything from paint remover, industrial soap, a few bathmats, curtain rods, and three packs of valances. Holy shit, she *was* magic.

"Well, little lady, I think the missus is gonna really like this. I'm thinking I can get these curtains up and surprise her with a new sewing room next time she runs off for her ladies meetin'. You know how them old birds gossip. That should give me at least a few hours to get everything to rights."

The tinkle of December's laugh teased the air. "I'm sure Mrs. Winchester will love it. But like you promised, if she thanks you with blueberry pie, you save me a slice."

"Will do, sweetheart. Hey, what's this? You doing kitchens now, Cord?"

They'd been selling kitchens for over a decade. Before he had a chance to answer, his employee of the minute stepped in.

"Cord has beautiful cabinets. Have you seen the catalogue?" She spun the binder to face Winchester. "Could you imagine how good Mrs. Winchester's muffins would taste with a new convection oven?"

The man frowned over the picture of the shiny state of the art appliance and Cord knew she'd lost him.

"This one of them electric ones?"

December leaned close and read the description. "Looks like it."

"We have gas—an old one. She's always complaining that if she don't check it every fifteen minutes the bottoms of her cakes burn. I bought her one of those fancy cake cuttin' wires to level them out and trim away the crispy parts. I'm bettin' she'd like this a bit more."

Holy fuck. If she sold this man an oven he'd kiss her.

"You know... Valentine's Day is just around the corner."

He grunted. "I got that covered. However, her birthday's in March. How much does one of these go for?"

Here we go.

"This one's listed for eight o'nine, but if you don't want stainless the same model in white is priced for only seven. You could also do black. What color's your refrigerator?"

"White."

"So you'd probably want it to match."

"Yeah, she gets riled up when I don't coordinate things. You should have seen the day I brought home sheets that weren't the exact blue of the bedspread." Old Winchester whistled. "I'm still hearing about that and that was back in ninety-four."

Cord watched as the small talk continued. She was amazing. Not only was she charming the pants off the town miser, she was glowing. Who *wouldn't* want to talk to her?

December had the gift of making the person

she addressed feel like the center of the universe. He was getting jealous of all the attention the old man was getting. How could Austin ignore such a charming woman who, to his thinking, was impossible to ignore? His mood darkened when he thought about how his friend was also successfully ignoring *him* lately.

When it came time to ring Winchester up, December struggled with the register. Cord leaned over her shoulder and told her which commands to key, breathing her in as though stocking up on her scent. He fought the urge to press closer, the way he'd fought other inappropriate desires—and succeeded.

Once she had the order processed, she handed off the receipt, and thanked Mr. Winchester for shopping at Bay's. She was a goddamn natural.

"And I'll let you know about that range, darlin'. Give me a day or two to think it over."

"Okay. And don't you go moving that chest of drawers without help. Call me if you can't find someone to do the heavy lifting."

The old man shook his head and laughed, probably finding the idea of little December lugging an antique chest of drawers as comical as Cord did.

Once the doors closed and they were alone, she pivoted and squealed. "I did it!"

Her arms shot out, nearly dislocating his back as she yanked him down into a hug and bounced. He couldn't help but laugh. "You sure did."

She broke away, her eyes alight with enthusiasm. "Did you see me? Oh, I worked him over real good! Not that I was trying to be manipulative," she quickly added. "Mrs. Winchester's going to love everything he bought! But still... that was...*liberating*. I think I have a gift for retail. I should start wearing pinky rings and gaudy suit jackets."

He chuckled. A natural gift for salesmanship, or...boobs? No, it was definitely more personality than anything else.

"You did great. But don't get your hopes up. Winchester's the cheapest man in town. Doesn't matter that he's got all that money. He doesn't spend a dime of it unless he has to."

By the end of the day, December found her niche. When she asked to take the catalogues home to study, he let her bundle them up, not expecting her to get too far on the inventory, but she was determined.

Each night she took home a new catalogue and each morning she arrived with much of the content committed to memory. He worried that the time she was dedicating to her new position was actually a way to avoid broaching the subject of her new job with her husband. When he asked where Austin was while she was studying kitchen cabinetry and the like, she always had the same answer—sleeping.

All evening? Every evening?

Nothing Ember said about her home life at the moment matched the way he remembered it to be, but he didn't doubt her honesty. The condition of her Jeep spoke for itself, and the amount of debt... He wasn't sure waiting until the end of the week to confront Austin was right. He needed to speak to his friend sooner than later.

As he carried in a new shipment of hand warmers, she was bagging up some complimentary paint stirrers for a customer.

"I think you're really going to like that finish." She handed over the receipt. "Take care. We'll call you when the faucet comes in."

As soon as the customer left, she pivoted, a smug grin on her face. "I believe, you, Mr. Bay, owe me lunch."

"Un-freaking-believable."

He'd foolishly bet her she wouldn't be able to market an overpriced line of spigots in the new catalogue they just received. They were beautiful, but the price was bonkers. He should have known better. She could sell a glass of water to a drowning man.

She buffed her nails on her apron. "I know. I'm pretty awesome. I think I'll have pizza. Oooh, no, I want to try the new Peking duck special over at Hung Lau. By the way, Mrs. Carmen called to thank us for talking her husband into buying the copper doorknobs. She said it's amazing what a big difference a little change can make."

Okay, yeah, she earned her free lunch. It was worth it just to see her smiling. He swiped a strip of paper from the receipt roll. "Okay, so that's one Peking duck special and an order of crow for me."

His pen slipped when she bumped him with her hip. "Don't be bitter. It's your profit. I'm just glad I found something I'm good at."

He frowned. That was the third time this week she'd made a comment like that. "Hey, you're good at lots of things."

She rolled her eyes, dismissing his compliment, which pissed him off. As she tried to walk away he grabbed her arm and foiled her escape. "December, you're good at lots of things."

"Okay," she laughed, the sound contaminated with sarcasm.

"I'm serious. Let me hear you say it."

Her face twitched as she glanced around. "Don't be ridiculous." Her smile remained, but a bit of self-consciousness reflected in her eyes.

"No one's here. Say it."

Color tinged her cheeks. "No. That's stupid."

"No. Hearing a girl like you put herself down is stupid. Now, say it. *I'm good at lots of things.*"

Her chin trembled as she stared up at him, eyes pleading and her smile absent. He knew he'd plucked a vulnerable nerve, but she didn't have to pretend with him. He needed to hear her say it, because thinking a girl as great as December could doubt herself in such a way broke his heart.

A silent debate waged between them until she finally breathed out the words in an almost silent whisper. "I'm good at lots of things."

He released his hold and nodded, satisfied. "Good. I'll order that faucet. Should be here by next Monday."

The shift in subject seemed to break her trance. "I'll call. I need practice anyway." She gathered the order slip and shifted toward the phone.

"Will you be okay here if I go pick up lunch?"

"Sure. I'll call your cell if I have a question."

"Okay."

As soon as he made it to his truck he ordered lunch and then drove in the opposite direction of the Hung Lau. Spurred by December's self-deprecation, he saw no point in wasting another minute to speak to his friend.

Ten minutes later he pulled in to Austin's driveway. The guy's truck hadn't moved since Saturday, but someone—likely December—had cleared off the newly fallen snow.

Rather than knock, he used the key wedged behind the porch light and let himself in to the house. The kitchen was spotless, but the living room was a disaster.

"Austin?"

His attention snagged on the couch where the blankets moved. Using the toe of his boot he tapped the lump. "Get up."

Austin's body shifted, unearthing from the stale scented blankets like a jetty in a dormant lake. "Cord?" His voice was gravelly, as if he hadn't spoken in days. "What the hell are you doing here?"

"I came to ask you the same question. Jesus, you look like shit."

The sour odor of day old beer was inescapable. Austin's typically handsome features wore lines of strain Cord wasn't used to seeing. Austin shifted into a seated position and a cookie wrapper fluttered to the carpet, landing in a sprinkling of beer tabs. Various cans lined the table like broken soldiers.

Austin scrubbed his hands roughly up and down his face where a beard had grown. "You hungry, man? I'm starved." He glanced toward the hall. "Ember!"

Cord's jaw locked. "She's not here."

"She's not? Where'd she go?"

Narrowing his eyes, Cord scowled at his best friend, resisting the urge to knock his teeth out. "Where the hell have you been, Austin? She's working."

"Working? Ember doesn't work anymore."

"Well, someone around here has to! Look at you. What the fuck are you doing?"

Austin stiffened, all friendliness gone. "What the fuck are you talking about? My wife doesn't work."

"No, more like your marriage doesn't work. She called you the day of the accident and you didn't even pick up—"

"*What the fuck are you talking about? What accident?*"

"Jesus, Austin!" His body trembled with bottled up rage. "Her fucking car drove off the road! I found her unconscious! Didn't you even notice the lump on her head?"

Austin jumped to his feet, swaying until he gained his balance, blood draining from his face. "No one fucking told me! Where the hell is my phone? Is she all right?"

Without thinking, Cord stepped forward and shoved him back on the couch. Getting right up-close and personal, he growled, "No, she's not all right! She was in a fucking accident, because you let her drive in the snow, in a ten-year-old piece of shit Jeep with bald tires. She could have died, you prick!"

Austin shoved back and Cord caught his best friend's wrist.

Through gritted teeth Cord snarled, "Go ahead. Push me. Give me one reason to come at you and I'll gladly beat some sense into your thick head." Releasing Austin with a scoff of disgust, he stepped back and stood at his full height. "Be a man. Get your shit in order, and talk to your *wife*."

Austin peered up at him, bloodshot eyes too telling of his fatigue and confusion. Cord experienced a curious sensation of pity and disgust, two things he'd never felt about his best friend. They ranked up there with other things he'd convinced himself were unpalatable, unacceptable.

"Talk to her and fix this," he snapped, giving one final warning, afraid if he stayed he might actually do damage. This wasn't the man he knew and admired. The one friend he loved above all others. He stomped out, slamming the door so hard it rattled in the frame.

It was a good thing Austin hadn't spewed excuses for his behavior, because Cord's temper was currently held in place by a very thin, fraying thread. He doubted he could have contained himself if Austin shirked off one bit of his accountability, and December wouldn't thank him for breaking her husband's face.

Five

December

THEY MUST HAVE RUN out of
something at home, because Austin called her
phone three times while she was helping customers. He hadn't left any messages and when
she called back it went right to voicemail. She
tried not to think about him while at work, but
he permeated her thoughts on the drive home.

The walk to their front door needed shoveling again and her back was killing her from
being on her feet all day. Annoyed, she parked
her Jeep by the garage and marched through the
piles of snow, confused by the sight of masculine
footprints. Maybe he actually considered going

somewhere today. Glancing back at his truck her hope dwindled. He hadn't gotten far. The thing was once again covered in snow and the tires were still packed in drifts.

The house was dark, but she knew something was up the second she stepped inside. The very air reeked of tension. "Austin?"

"Living room."

"Of course," she mumbled, as she stripped off her hat and coat. Stepping into the den she braced herself for whatever mood he was in today. He was on the couch but not in his usual lounging position. Marking his stiff demeanor, caution sparked in her belly.

"Hey."

He scowled, his face dark behind his scruffy beard. Even his looks were starting to change. Austin had always been in impeccable shape, but recently he'd let it all fall away. The changes to his physique were just another indicator of how much he'd come to neglect. She would never complain, because by the grace of some incredible god, he found all her bumps and jiggles attractive—or at least he used to.

She was five foot two and, when she ate well, had more ass and belly than boobs. Always shaped like a pear, she'd hoped nature would one day balance her out, but that never happened. She wore her hair longer to balance out her body

—and hide what she couldn't improve. Also because Austin loved her long hair—or used to.

So, yeah, even with the added ten pounds of beer gut and a desperate need for a shave, he still had her beat by miles. His light brown hair, coupled with soft brown eyes should have been unremarkable, but they weren't. He was gorgeous, intimidatingly so. His arms were cut from working outdoors and until now he'd usually maintained a year round tan. Even with his new, self-imposed, indoor life, his coloring was more alive than her pallid tone.

"Where you been?"

The tension knotting her shoulders was undeserved. There was no reason to be worried when she'd done nothing wrong. He was the one who should be spitting out explanations—and apologies—now that he was finally talking to her again. Yet the foreign concept of communicating with her husband made her uneasy.

"I...uh...got a job."

"Where?"

"Bay's Hardware."

Whatever was in his hand crumpled into a little ball and flew onto the table as he cursed. "I thought we talked about you working."

Gone was the slurred dialogue she'd become accustomed to over the past months. "We need the money, Austin."

His fingers tapped restlessly, those big hands no longer seeming as capable as they once were. All these slight physical changes on top of the many emotional shifts were slowly erasing the husband she loved and replacing him with a stranger she struggled to recognize.

"I'll get money."

His assurance brought zero relief. She no longer trusted him to be the follow- through man he'd always been. "How? You aren't taking any jobs—"

"You think I'm turning them down? There aren't any, Ember."

Refusing to shy away as he raised his voice, she lifted her chin. "Cord said he offered you a job."

"Fucking Cord. What, are you two best friends now?"

She stiffened. "No, but he's *our* friend. We could have used his help, Austin. Why didn't you tell me he offered you a position at the store?"

"Because I'm not a fucking clerk and I'll be damned if I work as his little gofer boy." He threw himself back against the cushion and glared, petulance and pained affront emanating from every pore.

Frustration tightened her chest until her throat constricted, making it difficult to breathe evenly. This was what she faced after all her efforts? "That's pride talking, Austin. You put your pride before *our* needs—needs you swore to always put first."

It was as if her words had fallen on deaf ears. "I don't want you working there."

Her jaw trembled. That job was the only thing that had brought her happiness in a long time. The customers appreciated her help. So did Cord. But most of all *they* needed the money, not that she'd reference their lack of funds again.

"I'm not giving up my job at the store. I like it."

He scoffed. "Maybe a little too much."

"Excuse me?"

"You know what I mean."

"No, I don't. Please elaborate." She was getting into it now, something best to avoid but she couldn't hold back.

He buttoned up, only parting his lips to take a swig of whatever he was drinking. Looked like soda, but she'd be willing to bet there was booze in the mix. This childish version of Austin wasn't a part of the man she knew, yet these infantile tantrums kept interfering in their home life. "Are you drunk?"

"No, I'm not fucking drunk. Don't change the subject."

"Then quit playing games. Say what you mean."

"No games, December. Pretty goddamn convenient it's Cord who offered you a job."

Okay, for sure there was no avoiding this confrontation. She wasn't a doormat. She might have taken this crap a few days ago, but since being forced to take back some control in her life she decided enough was enough.

Actions spoke louder than words and until he *showed* her he was capable of change she would no longer believe his empty promises. She wasn't doing this with him anymore.

Calmly, she said, "I'm confused. Is this about me going back to work or the fact that Cord was the one who offered me a job?"

"He doesn't need you feeding his ego."

What the hell was he talking about? The only ego in their way was Austin's. "He's your best friend!"

"Then where the fuck's he been, Ember? Where was he when I needed him?"

His logical brain was definitely on vacation, or maybe that childish perspective was more than temporary. "You have to *ask* for help, Austin. You can't sit around expecting it and then get mad when no one knows you're in need. And he offered you a job. Sounds like help to me."

"Jesus. I don't know which one of you is the bigger champion for the other. He doesn't need you defending him. Maybe I should just bow out and let you two ride off into the happy sunset of lumber and lawnmowers."

"What the hell are you talking about?" He'd never shown a jealous side before, especially not where Cord was concerned. What was there to be jealous about?

She couldn't fathom the root of such resentment. It seemed Austin was adamant the world suddenly owed him something and everyone else was to blame for his misfortune.

"Cord's always been our friend. He's still yours, but you shut everyone out. Why? It's bad enough that you don't talk to me, but it's totally unfair for you to try and squander the friendships I have left."

He rolled his eyes as if everything she just said was unfounded. "Do me a favor, Ember, find your own friends to bitch to about our personal life and leave my friends out of it."

A slick, oily sensation slithered through her stomach. He knew she was working with Cord, but she'd said nothing about confiding in him. "What?"

"Cord came here today on his high horse to tell me what a shitty husband I've been. If you have a problem...there's the door."

Shock, buffeted by pain, knifed through her. This was her *home*, a place she'd always considered her domain, her pride and joy that showcased her love and affection for her husband. Austin used to insist that, without her, it was just a house, that *she* made it a home. But her love was lost in these empty halls, his hate vanquishing it like a relentless enemy she was weary of fighting.

Fear kicked her heart rate up as it pulsed in her temples and at the base of her throat. She breathed unsteadily and took a staggering step back. "Are you telling me to leave?"

"If you're so unhappy..."

"If one of us is unhappy, we talk, Austin. How could you say that? The man I know would *never* tell me to leave!"

He shrugged, looking everywhere but at her, and agony choked her. "I've said my piece. I don't want you working there."

Her voice was a mere trembling of syllables linked together by sharp breaths as she struggled not to hyperventilate. "What about what *I* want? What *I* need? Do you even care anymore? We were losing our house—"

"Don't be dramatic."

"Look at the fucking mail! It's all there if you'd get off your ass and open it! We owe over five grand. Our electric was a minute away from being shut off. We can't afford food, yet you somehow manage to buy beer and booze! I can't live like this—"

"Then leave!"

Speechless, she blinked. Pain etched like acid around the edges of her already broken heart as his words echoed in the stunned silence.

"When did your love for me turn to hate?" She'd nearly whispered the question, yet it reached all corners of the room where her husband had taken up residence, the detritus of his current life strewn haphazardly around them.

Pinching the bridge of his nose, he sighed. "I don't hate you, December. I fucking hate myself."

Regardless of her physical toils, nothing made her as bone weary as this ongoing battle to urge her husband back to the wonderful man she remembered. Sighing, she said, "Yet I'm the one being punished. This isn't the life either of us wanted, Austin. It certainly isn't the one you promised me."

"I'll get a fucking job."

"I'm not just talking about work. Yes, money's necessary, but this is so much more than that and you know it." Her insides were hollow, but she sought the words and forced them out. "Austin...you don't...touch me anymore. It's like I repulse you or something."

He gaped, but any possible shame quickly morphed into anger as his brow lowered with a scowl. "You telling Cord about that too? About what we…what we do together?"

How dare he turn her gut-wrenching fear into a pissing contest? Humiliation had her arms protectively curling around her stomach as his words seared into her. "Leave him out of this."

"You brought him into it."

Did so. Did not. Just when she thought her life couldn't deteriorate further.

"Austin, please…"

"It's my job to work. You're supposed to be *here. That's* what we both wanted. Or so you said."

She couldn't take any more. The hurt, the loneliness, the pressure to fix this on her own, it all erupted out of her in an ugly rage.

"Then man up and assume your role! Find a fucking job! I've been here for you, as your wife and all that entails. *Wife* according to Austin. I'm your damn accountant, maid, chef, and lover —not that it matters to you anymore—but if you think I'm going to sit around and watch everything we've built wash away because you're too damn drunk or prideful to ask for help when we so desperately need it, you're insane."

"Oh, I'm insane? Why would I want to talk to someone who's always bitching about all the ways I disappoint her? And what the fuck does that even mean, *not that it matters to me anymore*?"

"Me, Austin. I'm referring to *me*. It's been almost a year since you acted like my husband."

"Bullshit."

"Really? Would you like to see my calendar?"

"What are you, keeping track?"

"I always do. It's part of being a woman. It's been since May."

"You're lying."

There was nothing more to say, nothing further to offer. His face twisted in disgrace and his scowl lowered. Was he thinking back to the last time they'd been intimate? The last time he actually showed an inkling of the virility he'd once defined himself by? Did he realize she spoke the truth?

"You don't even sleep in our bed anymore." God, it hurt to say that out loud.

His stare leapt to hers and the rage seeped away, replaced by remorse—or shame. It drilled a hole in her heart.

"It has nothing to do with you, December. I'm just..." He gestured helplessly. "Going through some shit."

Shit. Right. She didn't want to fight with him, but this was a fresh start she meant to finish. No point in ripping off the bandage again and again. Things had to get better.

"Maybe. Maybe not." Her gaze drifted to the floor. "I gave up trying to figure it out about six months after you stopped talking to me. My point is, you've been absent far too long, and for you to come down on me for taking on some much needed independence isn't fair. I was losing my mind stuck in this silent house. I'm keeping the job."

"December..."

Seconds ticked down and she debated which was worse, his silence or another promise he'd likely break. It was like living with a ghost. She could sense his presence, but not reach him when he was so close. She could hear him, but he wouldn't talk to her, or touch her, hold her. He was just there, passing through life on some journey she couldn't follow.

The same redundant pleas begged in her mind. *Please talk to me. Tell me how to fix this. What can I do to make it better? Tell me. I'll do anything to have you back. Please.*

His voice was low and gravelly. "I'll get better. I know I fucked up. I'll find a job and I'll fix this. I'll fix us."

It was the same thing he always said when they fought since he lost his job, but in a day or two they'd be right back where they were. She was truly convinced whatever this enemy was, it was bigger than the both of them. She didn't have the energy for blind faith anymore. His groundless guarantees had hurt her too many times.

Sighing, she turned toward the hall, speaking over her shoulder. "So you've said. In the meantime, I'll continue to work at the hardware store. I'm going to bed. Good night."

He didn't bother to respond, not that she expected it. Their pact of never going to bed angry had gone by the wayside along with many other promises.

Her long day had left her pleasantly tired, but now she was exhausted to the point of nausea. Reaching her room was paramount. She tossed her clothes in the direction of a hamper and clambered into bed.

Adept at trotting out all her thoughts and worries upon laying her head on the pillow, she usually picked through them in an attempt to seek a way out of the mess that was their life. But it was time she let that practice go and trusted she had things under control. Her diligence was her greatest weapon.

As she drifted off to sleep, she heard the bedroom door creak open. A frisson of dread caught her breath.

Through squinted eyes, she watched Austin

creep in, his big body silhouetted against the light from the hall. Part of her rejoiced at his return to their room, seeing it as the first sign that he did want to fix them, yet another part of her panicked at the intrusion.

The space they once shared together had become entirely hers, a private escape from his gloomy moods and overwhelming depression. It wasn't that she was without compassion. She'd tried to understand what he was going through, tried to be empathetic. But how many times could she reach into a cage only to have her fingers bit? As much as she wanted him there, her desire was banked by her fear of being hurt yet again.

She catalogued his movements with her eyes tightly closed, keeping her limbs still under the covers. Drawers slid open and closed, his footsteps muffled as he rounded the foot of the bed. Had there ever been a time when he'd crept into their room like a thief in the night, a territory he'd once dominated?

Her heart pounded in sick anticipation. *Stay. Go.* She wanted him there yet she didn't. He wasn't well. He wasn't himself. This was deeper than his employment situation and she wasn't qualified to solve such intangible problems. She wanted to fix this for them, and her failure to do so weighed heavily on her shoulders—another load to bear.

The mattress dipped as he climbed into bed and any hope of sleep vanished. She'd forgotten the sound of his breathing, and his once familiar scent was tainted with the sour odor of alcohol. She yearned to breathe deep and recover the reassuring aroma of the man she loved more than life itself.

He shifted closer and her mind recoiled. At some point over the past few months, indignation overrode her desperation. No matter how much she longed for physical affection, he'd lost the privilege, her open invitation to him revoked. Consent was only bestowed on those who were worthy of it and her natural desire to please was lost in a pile of broken bits of her battered pride.

Sighing into her pillow, her cheeks moistened with silent tears. She was sick of crying. Maybe after talking rationally about the reality of their situation they could take this step, but right now, after a juvenile fight, it solved nothing.

Rather than spoon her like before, he maintained his distance. Perversely, she resented that space, despite her earlier thoughts of too little too late and her ever-present fears of too much too soon. If he touched her she could reject him

—or not. But it would be her choice, something lacking of late and fueling her bitterness.

The ache she'd carried around for months multiplied until she was weeping in earnest. She was losing her mind, wanting to push him away as much as she needed him to pull her close.

Why couldn't he just grab hold of her, turn her, and kiss her like he used to? Couldn't he hear her muted sniffles and muffled sobs?

Quietly, she rolled to her side and faced him. Thin bands of moonlight filtered through the blinds to stripe his face, softening the damage wrought by too much alcohol and bitterness.

He was already sound asleep, and her resentment flared. How could anyone sleep that much? Why did their worries only keep *her* awake when he should be tirelessly seeking solutions?

Having the chance to study him up close and unguarded, she once again registered all the physical changes in him. Her chest pinched as she thought about the tedium of fixing her hair and ensuring her appearance was flawless—for him. And he couldn't even shower and shave regularly.

Deep down, she had to believe his avoidance of intimacy wasn't about her. Austin liked sex, and a lot of it. She'd always been available, because his driving need matched hers, his strength and authority the perfect counterpart to her gentle grace. But if he wanted it elsewhere she supposed—no matter how much it hurt to admit—he could easily find it. Except he never left the couch, or the house aside from his short trips to buy beer.

The booze had not only numbed him to their financial situation but also quashed his libido. Whatever she had to offer, it wasn't enough.

And there went another chip of her heart, falling into the abyss of broken promises and lonely nights. A collection of shattered pieces hid behind her ribs. But she loved him to a fault, so she kept sweeping the shards into a pile, certain one day he'd glue them back together.

How long could a person survive on mere memories of a beautiful marriage before they admitted to failure and gave up?

Resolutely, she pushed all her musings aside and sought the oblivion of slumber.

Falling deeper into her exhaustion, she flinched at the pressure building between her legs and her eyes opened on a gasp.

"Hey, baby."

The fresh scent of soap competed with her husband's fragrance of late, but a warm, familiar heat bloomed in her belly. She frowned as he slid up her body, his freshly shaven jaw pressing against her throat.

"Let me..."

The weight of his hard body pressed her deeper into the mattress and a stunned yearning unfurled inside of her. "You have no idea how long I've wanted to take you. Tell me you're still mine, Ember. I need to hear it."

As he awaited her assurance, he gently pulled down the covers and she shivered. He lifted her arms, pressing them into the pillows, so dominant, so Austin.

"Tell me," he repeated.

Despite her earlier struggles to acclimate their new roles, the truth remained. "I'm yours. Always yours, Austin."

Stretching his fingers up her arms, he blanketed her body with his. Her toes pointed as her legs extended with a delicate roll of her hips. He was hard and the press of his cock against her hip healed more damage to her shattered self-esteem than any words could.

His palm trailed down her arm to her ribs as he plumped her breast in the L of his fingers. "That's right. All mine."

Pulling back the strap of her nightgown, his mouth closed over her nipple and her head tipped back, her spine arching toward him as she gasped at the overwhelming contact. His hips rolled, dragging over hers possessively, his erection a mute testament to how much she aroused him, removing all of her doubts.

He exposed her further, pushing her nightgown to her hips as his fingers trailed below the blankets, his mouth leaving wet kisses on her breasts. "Open for me."

Her knees parted as he lifted his weight ever so slightly and his fingers slid into her panties, delving between her folds and ripping a gasp of pleasure from her lungs. He fed his digits deep, zeroing in on her most sensitive spots.

"It's been too long," he whispered, gently fucking his fingers in and out.

His thumb grazed her clit and her entire body shivered. So starved for the slightest affection, she was an overloaded fuse ready to blow.

"Austin," she breathed, her hips rocking into his hypnotic touch.

A strange fear eroded her pleasure. If she came, would he stop? She didn't want him to let her go. She needed him to stay with her. Hold her through the storm and sheltering her long afterward.

"Please," she begged. "I need you."

His hips wedged between her thighs, stretching her anticipation reed thin. "You need me," he whispered as the blunt tip of his cock parted her slit. "Is this what you want?" he teased.

"Please," she begged again, her hands itching to hold him to her, but she knew her surrender was more of a lure to him. "Yes. You always know what I want."

He edged inside of her by a mere inch and her lips parted, bated breath balancing her on a razor's edge of pleasure. His tongue swiped at her nipples. "God, you're gorgeous."

Her wrists turned outward as her hands twisted in the pillows. Cool air danced over her chest as he made her wait in suspended need for another torturous second. It was *this*, the waiting, the intense anticipation, the absolute surrender to his dominant nature that undid her in too many ways to count.

No man had made her feel the way he did, as if he knew all the hollow parts of her soul and could fill them with love. Her breath trembled past her lips as the moment feathered out and her need burned to a scorching degree. It was here, in their home, in the silent moments of intimacy, that he owned her, body, heart and soul.

"There's my girl," he whispered, sliding deep to deliciously stretch her, delivering a sense of homecoming only he could bring.

She sighed and panted as he held steady,

buried deep inside of her. It had been so long, she feared it would never be the same. But this was how it had always been, intense to the point that all vanity was stripped away and only the raw desire to satisfy each other existed.

His head lowered to her shoulder as his broad form twitched with a shudder of pleasure. "Jesus, Ember, how the fuck did I ever deny us this?"

Her fingers itched to touch him, but she waited until he gave her permission. He thrust his hips, pushing into her quickly as if he couldn't bear the slightest distance between them.

"Touch me, baby. I need to feel you."

Her finger threaded through his hair, over his broad shoulders and down his back as he thrust hard, taking the edge off of so many lonesome nights. His grip tightened as he kissed her neck and shoulders, slowly lifting his chest from hers.

"You're it for me, Ember. Only you."

His words were a balm to her shredded heart and her vision blurred and she shut her eyes as she drew in what felt like her first heartfelt breath in months. "Only us."

His lips softly brushed hers and she smiled against his kiss, laughing despite her tears of joy. "I'm so glad you're back."

"I thought you needed space, but I was wrong. Give me time, Ember. He'll come around. So will I. "

Like a bucket of ice being dumped over her, her blood chilled and her body tensed. Too much registered at once. She could still feel his weight on top of her, his length filling her...only it wasn't her husband's whiskey brown eyes staring down at her, but deep blue ones that should never see her like this.

"Austin!"

She jerked fully awake at the sound of her own scream, unsure if she'd dreamed her voice calling for her husband or actually spoken aloud. Shoving out from under the covers, she caught her breath and stumbled out of bed.

Her eyes winced at the bathroom light, but she needed the glaring shock of reality to wipe away the cobwebs of sleep. Blinking into the mirror, she panted and caught her breath.

What the hell had that been? She'd *never* dreamt about Cord in a sexual manner. And what had he said to her? She couldn't recall as the dream was already fading.

Sudden disappointment hit her like a cannonball to the stomach when the implication of her husband's return had, yet again, been snatched away, leaving nothing but cold reality.

Her head dropped between her shoulders. It was just a dream.

Biting her lips between her teeth, she blinked back her tears and straightened her spine. Shutting off the light, she quietly cracked the door. Austin snored softly on his side of the bed, still in the same position he'd been in when he first settled beside her, still unshaven and looking like a stranger.

Slowly approaching the bed, she rolled to her side so as not to face him, but additional hints of truth crowded in anyway. There was no scent of clean soap, only the sour stench of stale beer. The cold chasm of distance between them needled painfully at her backbone and she shut her eyes, curling further to the edge of the mattress and gripping the corner of the blanket tight.

This was her reality. Her dream—minus the strange twist at the end—was her past.

Six

December

DECEMBER'S MIND gradually roused as darkness shifted to light and the sun slowly filtered through the curtains. A draft of cool air teased her senses and she opened her eyes after a long and unsettled night of broken sleep and disjointed dreams.

He was gone. Her battered heart couldn't withstand the constant jabs, hitting her over and over again in the same soft spots. Every day, his abandonment stabbed deeper than the day before. He couldn't give her one goddamn night in their bed before he was back on the couch again.

The physical hunger, the emotional strain,

the decay of their friendship, it all hurt, but his disregard hurt more than anything else. Austin knew her better than anyone. He knew the life she had before him and how much she'd hated the instability of it. His promises of a safe and secure home were what made her fall so in love with him. And they both knew that security was more than just a roof and some walls.

Rolling to her back she stared at the ceiling, letting her disappointment wash over her. More than anything, she feared he'd leave her no choice but to walk away, pitting himself against her dignity in a way that no illusion of authority could overrule. With everything she'd surrendered willingly, it had been her choice to give and her right to rescind.

Traveling throughout her childhood from state to state like a pack of gypsies left December with plenty of vulnerable traits, but she never mastered hiding them effectively. She knew too well what it was like to go to bed with the illusion of permanence only to wake and find everything changed. It was a pain she'd become quite familiar with throughout her childhood, her parents, Rona and Misha, never giving her much notice before ripping away the slight stability she'd grown used to the day before.

Austin knew better than anyone how much she hated her undependable life and how any sort of uncertainty awakened her scariest demons, which made his unpredictable behavior all the more hurtful. He'd opened up her world, rescuing her from the erratic life of a drifter to show her stability could be a reality. And then, with his recent actions that stability had vanished.

She was trapped in her own foolish hope. Last night he'd told her to get out and it gutted her. She wasn't ready to walk away, not from all that they had. Deep down, she still believed the good times far outweighed the bad, but the rankings were drawing closer together and she wasn't sure how much longer she could honestly live like this. She'd thought her life of relying on undependable people was over.

Setting her jaw, she rolled out of bed and marched into the bathroom. She irritably brushed her teeth, and barely took the time to splash water on her face and smooth her hair. When she made the coffee, she made only enough for herself and used the last of the milk on purpose.

Her pacing around the kitchen halted at the sight of the empty bottle of rum on the counter. Anger subsided to make room for concern.

Jesus, when had he drunk all of that? How long ago had he graduated from beer to hard stuff? Her fingers trembled as she picked up the empty container, rocking it as though it was one of those dolly bottles that miraculously refilled with liquid when tipped.

She needed to talk to Cord. This was bad. Someone could die from drinking that much high proof alcohol in short periods of time, couldn't they?

Dread gripped her with icy fingers, as the house suddenly seemed beyond silent. Stuttering breaths filled her lungs as she stole through the hall toward the den. Her feet paused at the threshold as her unblinking stare landed on his limp arm where it draped onto the floor.

Dear God.

Creeping into the room, her pace faltered the closer she came to the couch. Terror froze her heart, slowing her movements despite the screaming need to assure herself he was breathing.

Staring down at his still body, she studied his face, the skin waxen and motionless above the stubble. The room whirled as she hovered soundlessly. It wasn't until air whistled between his parted lips and his chest rose that she allowed oxygen into her own lungs.

She skittered backward, nauseated with relief as her hand drifted to her throat. Too intense. She couldn't deal.

Clutching her coat and keys in shaking

hands, she rushed out of the house, seeking the sanctuary of work for a few hours. She struggled into her coat and flung herself onto the cold seat of the Jeep, stabbing the keys into the ignition.

Gripping the wheel tightly, she quit thinking —and remembering—and made the rest of the drive on autopilot. When she got to the shop her hands grabbed for the door and missed, her fingers still trembling so fiercely they were useless. Trying again, she wrenched it open. Quickly stashing her items behind the register, she donned her apron and went to find Cord.

He was in the lumber aisle shoving a large slab of wood onto a shelf. Her steps faltered as she caught sight of his muscled arms stretching the fitted sleeves of his gray t-shirt. A sliver of toned flesh flashed above his jeans as his t-shirt rode up his tight abdomen. A sharp shiver teased her insides as her dream flashed in her mind's eye and she quickly shoved the images away, along with the sense of him inside of her. Not Cord. Austin. It was just a meaningless dream.

Shaking off the jolt to her senses and the disconcerting heat in her belly, she swallowed. "Cord?"

The board slid into place. "Hey, kiddo. Is it eight already?"

"I'm early. Do you have a minute?"

"Got lots of minutes." He brushed off his

hands, slapping them roughly together. "What do you need?"

"I'm worried about Austin."

His expression immediately turned serious and a bit guarded. "I don't know if I'm the guy you should ask to talk to him, if that's what you're after. He's sort of pissed at me right now."

"I know you went to see him yesterday when you went to pick up lunch."

"He told you?"

"Yes." There was no need to tell Cord how nasty Austin had been about the visit and the undeserved accusations he made. "I think Austin's drinking too much—no. I *know* he is, but I don't know what to do."

He drew in a slow breath as if processing this possibility. "Austin always was the kind of guy who liked a beer after work, but without a job to fill his days he may be hitting it a little hard. Did you say something to him about it?"

"Yes. I mean, I make little comments here and there when he spends money on beer that can be better spent on other things, but I never really mention how much he's consuming."

"How much is he drinking?"

"He finished a bottle of rum in one night— at least I think one night. I don't remember seeing that bottle before." The thought rankled and her fists flexed. Knowing Cord was watching her, she hid her hands in her apron, hiding away her uncertainty.

"A fifth?"

She was a wine from the box sort of girl. "How much is a fifth?"

He held up his hands about six inches apart. "They're the little bottles."

"No. More than that. It was a big bottle, like a wine bottle, but square."

Cord frowned. "Does he do that a lot?"

"I don't know. Taking out the trash is the one thing he still does around the house—most weeks. I don't usually see the recycling, but..." Her mind skipped over the times of late Austin had forgotten it was trash night and the grotesque amount of cans and bottles over-flowing the canister. She bit her lip. "Yes. He does it a lot."

Austin had always drank, but it had never been a problem. He was usually so conservative about over indulging and loved control too much to surrender it to anyone or anything. But he'd changed.

It was time she accepted this change and called it what it really was. Not only was her husband living in denial, she was too, thereby enabling him to carry on like this by skirting the reality. This wasn't a few nights of overindulgence. He had a problem with alcohol.

"Shit." Cord rubbed the back of his neck. "You should try to talk to him about it, but leave your finances out of it."

Her back tensed all the way to her neck. The slow fade of her denial told her this conversation would inevitably come, but she'd done her best to avoid it, praying the situation might fix itself. "I plan to, but I was hoping..." *For a miracle?*

"What?"

"I'm scared." The words fell from her lips, bearing more truth than she consciously realized.

"Scared? Of what?"

Her neck heated. "He just hasn't been himself lately and any time I say something to him he acts like I'm horrible and all I do is criticize him."

"Well, if he isn't giving you things to praise, that's on him."

Despite the truth of his comment, it wasn't helping. She didn't know what she expected Cord to do for her. He'd already done enough to help them. This wasn't his responsibility.

"You're right. I'll talk to him tonight."

When she turned he caught her arm. "Hey, December, if you want me to say something to him, I will. I'm just not sure that's the right move."

She was overwhelmed with trying to figure

out the correct approach to dealing with her husband. Every day she was more worn down than the last. "No. It's my place to talk to him."

"Ember, you know Austin would never hurt you, right? I know he can be a mean motherfucker when he's in one of his moods, but he loves you. He'd never put you on the receiving end of that. You're his world."

She would have whole-heartedly agreed a few months ago, but now she wasn't so sure. Maybe it was something only a married person could understand. She took *all* of Austin. Austin at his best and Austin at his worst. *That* was marriage. Except now the worst seemed infinite—and unpredictable.

She thanked Cord again and returned to the front of the store, aware he stared after her. The day dragged, unlike the previous ones, and with each passing hour her worries increased.

She constantly wondered what Austin was doing. Was he awake? Drinking? Sleeping it off? Regardless, he hadn't answered the phone any of the four times she called. Each missed call stung a little more so she forced herself to stop all together.

At four-thirty, Cord showed up at the register. "Here you go, your first slice of bacon to bring home."

"What?"

He slid a stiff piece of paper across the counter. "It's payday."

"Oh, yay!" She glanced at the check and choked. Seeing he was already walking away, she shouted, "Stop right there, Cordovan Charles."

He stilled and shivered. "I hate when you middle name me."

"Tough. If you don't explain this right now I'll tack on the last name too."

"Explain what?"

"This," she said, mashing her index finger on the dollar amount of the check. "I'm not taking this."

"Why not? It's all calculated properly. There's your hourly rate, all the deductions are listed clearly, I've applied a hundred to your debt, and the rest is yours."

"What cashier makes that much?"

"Um, you."

"No."

"December Skye Lockwood hyphen Garret, that's the going rate here at Bay's Hardware, so yes, you certainly are accepting it."

Her nose twitched at the sound of her ridiculous name, gifted to her by the two burned out hippies who created her. But she wasn't distracted or intimidated by his use of it.

"You're full of shit. Print me a new check with the hourly rate you pay the college kids and

I'll accept it. Otherwise I'm not cashing this and my family will have to go without bacon, because you're being a stubborn ass."

"*I'm* stubborn? Do you think those college kids work half as hard as you do? Consider the extra your commission for all the sales you made this week."

"Come on, Cord! You know I can't accept this."

The doors opened and a woman pushing a double stroller ambled in, not paying them any mind. She wandered off toward the lighting section.

Cord rounded the counter and gently gripped her arms. "Don't be stubborn, December. Take the money. You worked hard and I know that's close to what you made at the bank. You really helped me out this week, believe it or not. Don't be too prideful. Humble suits you better," he whispered.

"I didn't make this at the bank."

"So it's a few dollars over your old hourly rate. Take the money."

She looked at the check. It was almost half their mortgage. "I hate you."

He pressed his lips to her forehead and whispered, "You love me. You brought me toilet paper."

Shutting her eyes, her shoulders sagged as she

inhaled his woodsy scent. It nourished her, feathering comfort across her raw nerves. Then a fleeting shard of last night's dream made her step away. "Fine. But that means I'm tacking interest onto the loan. I'll make this even somehow."

"No, you won't." A cold, wet finger poked into her ear and she jerked back.

"Ew! You're disgusting!" Repulsed, she tried to remove the lingering sensation of a wet-willy with the bunched up cuff of her shirt. "What are you, twelve?"

"I told you I'm a child."

"Now I have to go disinfect my ear." She marched toward the bathroom, her heart again warm with gratitude.

"You know I'm sexy! Only the pretty girls get those sort of moves!" he shouted, and she laughed, perhaps for the first time that day.

She turned off the Jeep in front of the house and slumped on the sagging faux leather waiting for...something. Though working helped her state of mind and provided an escape from reality, returning home made her life seem harder.

Cold air seeped into the car, weighing down her limbs. She dreaded what she might find in the house and stayed staring at the façade, searching fruitlessly for a sign. Thinking of all the possibilities and the right response to each potential situation kept her in lockdown.

You won't know until you get in there. Stop wasting time.

With a reluctant huff, she clambered out of the vehicle and trekked her way through the snow. When she stepped inside, the house smelled different and she stilled.

Holy God! Fire!

She ran to the kitchen, seeking the source, and shivered with a spike of adrenaline. The crank window over the sink was ajar and the stale stench of smoke filled the air, though no smoke was visible.

"Austin?"

Sifting through the trash she found a burnt—no, singed—bag of microwavable popcorn. How long had he cooked it? She'd never seen a bag actually catch fire. The stink of smoke would have to be tolerated. Heat was too expensive to waste and the kitchen was freezing.

Biting off her glove, she cranked the window closed with jerky impatience. Tying up the trash bag, she carried it to the back porch. The overflowing recycling bin spoke volumes.

"Austin?" Her tone was fraught with anxiety but tempered with frustration. Music roared from some distant part of the house, vibrating the ceiling with heavy bass notes.

As she made her way up the stairs, she heard a familiar song. Collective Soul's *December* emanated from the spare room on the third floor. The volume rattled the pictures on the wall and she absentmindedly straightened one.

She pushed the door open and stood at the threshold without entering. Her husband lounged on the floor, scattered pictures from their earlier years surrounding him, a half filled bottle of Jack in his hand. His expression was anything but welcoming as he looked up at her.

She'd once liked the tune, years ago when she'd first heard it, but now...having her husband glare at her from a drunken stupor as he sloshed his way down memory lane and lip synched the words...not so much.

Stepping inside, she bent and yanked the cord of the old CD player from the wall, cutting off the noise.

"Hey! I was listening to that."

"Having fun?" What possessed him to go through these old boxes? And who was cleaning up this mess?

His fingers twisted, fanning out a few old candid shots of them from several summers back. "Not really. We're getting old."

"Thanks. I was just thinking, how could I

possibly feel worse about myself?" She snapped her fingers. "Aging. That always works."

His fingers coasted over their young, smiling faces. "You're still beautiful."

Her breath sucked in, tightening her chest. He had no idea how much she needed to hear him say that, to know he still found her remotely attractive. Her tear ducts flooded with pent up emotion. Fucking tears. Were they always going to be her go-to reflex when words failed to appropriately sum up her pain?

She blinked until her vision cleared, hopefully before he saw the tears, but her neglected heart clung to his comment. "You still think I'm pretty?"

He scowled at her, as if her question was baseless. "Of course, I do. What kind of twisted question is that?"

Was he living on another planet? Didn't he see what was happening to them? Her back pressed into the wall as she slowly slid to the floor. Fingers reaching for the closest stack of photos, she involuntarily smiled as memories overflowed from some protected place in her mind. "This is when we visited that B&B in Connecticut."

He chuckled and shut his eyes as he took a swig from the bottle. "Those people were so weird. I'll never go back there."

She laughed. "They weren't weird. They were hospitable."

"They were lurkers. Every corner I turned they were there, waiting with a towel or a pitcher of something. That place was the Twilight Zone."

"You liked it."

"I liked my naked roommate."

Her mind recalled the tacky floral wallpaper that clashed with the overdone Victorian curtains and she giggled. "Remember how squeaky the bed was?"

His teeth flashed beneath his beard. "Remember when we broke it?"

She snorted. "Whether we wanted to go back or not, I don't think we'd be welcome."

"They wouldn't let us leave and the next morning all we wanted to do was hightail it out of Crazyville before they noticed the bed."

It had been impossible to keep a straight face as the innkeeper insisted on giving her the recipe of the breakfast she'd politely complimented. "I never did make that egg casserole."

"Your eggs are better anyway."

He pinched her toe through her boot and she stilled, her senses cautiously exploring what was probably the first show of spontaneous intimate contact in months. It should have made her happy, but all she felt was sadness.

"What's happening to us, Austin? We haven't laughed like that in ages."

"Don't." He pulled away his hand. "Don't fucking spoil it."

Her stomach flipped, teetering between courage and fear. "Why? Because we might admit something neither of us are ready to face? Because we might be honest about what's actually happening here?"

His voice remained soft as it pitched into a singing tone. *"Don't worry 'bout, don't speak of—"*

"I hate that song."

"You used to like it."

Silence descended and time crept by. Her gaze crawled over the photos scattered on the floor. Those memories seemed a lifetime ago. Why torture herself with proof of how they'd once been? Remembering made the present all the more difficult.

"Remember this one?" He reached for the Bush CD.

A sad nostalgia filled her. "Oh, yes."

"Play it." He nudged the CD across the floor, closer to her.

Everything inside of her insisted she not touch the album. It held too much emotion, too many passionate flashbacks, too much reality in the face of all that had changed.

"I can't."

His brow creased. "Why?"

Swallowing back the pain, she shut her eyes. She was so fucking sick and tired of crying. "I can't walk down memory lane right now, Austin. I just...can't."

His clothing shifted and the CD player sprang open. The cord pulled through her fingers as he took it. "Do you remember the number?"

Ten. She kept quiet, as though the silence could arm her against the auditory ambush he was about to unleash.

"It's ten." Of course he knew it, too.

The rough guitar riff sounded and she breathed in what she feared would be her last breath. Keeping her eyes closed, she sensed him creeping closer until he too sat with his back to the wall. His breath, tinged with whiskey, puffed over her ear, and he whispered the slow lyrics of *Glycerine* against the thumping cello and whining strings.

Tender memories turned torturous in her mind. The first time they made love, tucked away in her narrow bed, rose petals sticking to their sweaty skin. Her shoulders trembled under the barrage of sensual images and the recollection of his assertive, loving touch, how right it felt when he finally filled her to the core.

It was a rather sad song, now that she thought about it outside of the moment. Whoever the artist was singing to, he'd lost her. Did Austin understand that too?

As he echoed the verse proclaiming to have treated her badly, she turned inward to the sound of her heart, certain another chip had just fallen into the mess behind her battered ribs. That's what ribs were for, right? A cage to catch the pieces of a crumbling heart?

His fingers caught her chin and slowly turned her face. She fought his touch for only a second, then gave in, blinking up at him. His brown irises shimmered back.

"I love you, Ember. You're my heart. Don't hate me."

A broken sob whispered past her lips, as her ribs tightened, hugging all the broken shards.

"I could never hate you, Austin. I'm sad, because I miss you. I don't know how to be without you and I feel like you've left me to go somewhere I can't follow."

"I'm right here, baby. Right here."

His lips traced over hers, soft like a feather's touch. She couldn't stem her tears, but he didn't seem to mind. His mouth gently played over hers as her mind gathered all of those broken pieces and mentally held them out to him like some sort of pathetic offering.

Had they gone back to start? Her comfort levels reset to a time where she wasn't sure how to be intimate with him. Everything was different, from the coarseness of his beard scratching her cheeks, to the scent of his throat. She couldn't even figure out where to put her damn hands, yet she was viscerally aware of every awkward place they rested.

"You're so hairy."

"I'll shave," he whispered.

The potent flavor of whisky assaulted her the moment he pressed his tongue into her mouth and she drew back.

"What?" He frowned.

"You...you taste like Jack."

He chuckled. "How do you know what Jack's kisses taste like?" When he went in for more she turned her face. She hated whiskey, everything about it, the flavor, the scent, what it did to people.

He made an exasperated sound and jerked back. "What's the problem, Ember? I'm trying to kiss you."

"You taste like whisky. I don't like it."

"Maybe you don't like *me*."

This new, passive aggressive way he twisted things to make her feel guilty was really starting to get to her. "I love you, Austin, but you drunk isn't one of my favorite things."

"I'm not drunk."

"You drank half a bottle of Jack. How does anyone do that and not get drunk?"

He sat back and swept his hand across a pile of pictures, sending photos scattering across the floor. "Jesus, Ember, you complain we never have sex and I try to kiss you and you get disgusted. What the fuck?"

Indignation had everything inside of her clenching tight as she prepared for battle. "What's disgusting is that you have to be half a bottle deep to even kiss me!" Shoving her palms against the wall she hoisted herself off the floor.

"Where are you going?"

"Where else? Bed. Alone."

"Oh, that's just great! Why don't you call your friend Cord and tell him how fucked up our marriage is? I'm sure he's just dying to hear the latest!"

Aaaaannnd, he was back to pinning the blame elsewhere. Turning on her heel, she towered over him. Something ugly deep inside of her unraveled, and came spewing out like a demon unleashed after ten long months of being caged.

"*Fuck you, Austin!* Cord's been a better friend to me in the past week than you've been in the past year! I was in an *accident* and you never even asked if I'm okay! Even now, you'd rather act like it didn't happen, like none of this is real when the truth is, the reality is *killing* me!"

"You never told me about the accident! I had to hear about it from Cord—*your hero!*"

"Yeah, well, he saved both our asses that day! You don't have a clue. You'd rather sit up here in an empty room imagining the people we no longer are. I drove off the road because I was *crying*—as usual—because after a morning of waking up and cleaning up *your* mess, I had to go around town begging for fuel so we didn't freeze to death in the house we're holding onto by the skin of our teeth!"

"I knew it! This is all about money!"

The world stilled. Everything paused as gravity released its tenuous hold and she simply hovered for a moment, catching her breath in some foreign place on the border of insanity. Austin glared, wordlessly daring her to justify herself.

When she finally collected herself enough to speak, her voice was so shrill she wouldn't have been surprised if the windows shattered. *"Don't you dare make me out to be some materialistic person! I don't care about money and you know it! I care about keeping a shelter over our heads and food in our fridge and fuel in the goddamn boiler! Fucking survival!"*

Something unstoppable unleashed in her

and she couldn't reel it back in but she managed to modulate her tone. To wield each word as a hammer in the hope it would sink in.

"How could you even imply this is solely about money? This is about *us*, plain and simple. It's about your inability to take less than what you think you deserve, because your fragile ego can't handle it. It's about your inability to be the husband I need, because you lost your job. People lose their jobs every day, Austin. It takes a *man* to get over the burn and brush himself off so he can try again. But you wouldn't know anything about that, because you'd rather spend ten months pissing your life away watching old DVDs through the empty end of a bottle."

She panted, her arms trembling fiercely. Austin stared wide-eyed at her, his mouth worked but nothing emerged. Well, he was going to finally hear all that she'd been trying to say for the past several months of his decline. She was done bottling her feelings up to protect him.

"You're so damn tied up in your own pity party, you're pushing everyone who loves you away. You barely even speak to me anymore unless you can't find something. *How about finding your wife?* Or how about your best friend? No, you'd rather villainize all of us. Did you ever stop to wonder how it is you're sitting here playing your old music in a warm house? You can thank

Cord for that! You know, the friend you can't find one good quality in—"

"*What?*" he roared.

She never saw a man spring to his feet so fast, drunk or not. He towered over her, face flushed, eyes livid, and she took a quick step back.

"*Do not* tell me you took money from him. I swear to God, Ember—"

"I took four thousand dollars from him."

Breathing heavily, she held his hard stare. She wouldn't lie if he was finally asking for the truth. His mouth snapped shut and his chest rose as he drew in a labored breath. Whisky scented air wreathed around them, an ominous miasma.

His words slithered through clenched teeth. "Get out."

She recoiled against the wall. "Excuse me?"

"*Get out!*" he shouted. "I can't look at you."

It wasn't the tone of his voice or the rage in his eyes. It was his words. *I can't look at you.* Agony twisted her being and wrung her soul dry. It would have hurt less had he kicked her in the ribs.

Her knees trembled as she gripped the handle of the door. Her righteous rage faded away, replaced by a desperate need to convince him she'd done what needed to be done as their last resort.

"Austin—"

"I said, get out!"

At the venomous snap of his voice she stumbled back, his words carving into her heart with the subtlety of an embedded cleaver. Still, she tried to reason with him. "You're not getting it—"

"I get it! I get it just fine. You couldn't depend on me so you went running to Cord, told him all our personal business, and he swooped in with his big bag of money and saved the day. Imagine that, you batted those big brown eyes at him—"

"It wasn't like that!"

He shoved past her, nearly knocking her into the wall. She followed him into their bedroom as he yanked open drawers, throwing his clothes into a pile. Now *he* was leaving?

They'd never fought like this and she didn't know what to do. Her first instinct was to call Cord, but that definitely wouldn't help in this situation. It struck her there was no one else to call. When had her world dwindled to just Austin? Just as they'd retreated from Cord, the rest of their circle of friends had been held at bay by the inability to reciprocate. They couldn't afford to host a party, or even dinner, let alone go out someplace. And then there was Austin's increasingly volatile behavior and anger toward everyone.

Grabbing his arms, she tried to still him, but he was too strong and deflected every touch. "Austin, stop it! This isn't us. Will you please just listen to me?"

"I'm leaving."

"You can't leave. You've been drinking."

"Like you care."

"I do care!" She was sobbing uncontrollably and couldn't seem to stop, couldn't stop him either. "Please! I love you. Don't do this. I'll give it all back."

"It's too late now. I'm sure you two had a big old laugh at what a failure I am."

"No! God, Austin, Cord's concerned, that's all—"

He spun so fast she shrank back and lifted her arm in self-defense. Mortification burned through her at the action.

He stilled and laughed coldly. "What? He's got you scared of me now? Poor, unstable Austin fell down. Who's going to put him back together again?" Shaking his head, he spat, "Fuck you both."

"Please, Austin." She grabbed his shirt and begged him to listen. "Stop and think for a minute—"

This time when he turned on her he didn't back down. Through gritted teeth, he snarled, "Get. Off."

Her grasp on his shirt fell away.

I can't look at you...Get off...

She stepped backward, feeling with one hand until the door met her flailing fingers.

The hatred that flashed in his eyes would haunt her for a long time, possibly forever. They were spiraling out of control and she couldn't get him to see reason. Like a frightened rabbit, she turned and bolted down the steps to the main floor. Her fingers sifted through the pockets of his coat until they closed around jagged metal. *Keys.*

Once she had them, she raced to the kitchen, and found his spare set. She couldn't let him drive in his condition. Darting back to the entryway, she collected her coat, and fled. She wouldn't return until he was dried out, sober, and ready to talk, however long it took.

Seven

Cord

CORD HOVERED at the edge of the kitchen, keeping the catatonic woman on his couch in his peripheral. Tears still dripped from her swollen eyes.

"Answer the fucking phone," he hissed, keeping his words low, as Austin's voicemail picked up again. "It's Cord. Call me back. I have your wife here, sitting on my couch—*crying!* Fucking crying, man." He huffed. "Pick up the goddamn phone."

Pocketing his phone, he collected the mug of tea—who knew he had tea—and carried it out to December. "I made you tea."

She said nothing. Her gaze appeared unfocused, yet unmoving. The mug clicked as he set it on the coffee table. Sighing, he lowered himself to the couch beside her. "Wanna talk about it?"

Nothing.

I'm going to kill you, Austin.

"Why don't you have some tea?"

Wasn't tea supposed to have all sorts of healing powers? Girls used it for cramps and other female problems. Maybe he should find chocolate or ice cream. If he'd known he was going to be Breakdown Headquarters, he would've stocked up on something more than tomato soup. He hated that he didn't know what to do.

This was the second fucking time she was melting down in his house—and the cause was the same. Fucking Austin.

Abruptly, her head dipped and her crying became audible, little whimpers that tore at him and made him want to strangle his friend. He awkwardly patted her shoulder. "There. There."

There, there? What the fuck did that even mean?

Her sobs grew louder and her entire body shook. Tightening every muscle in his face, he gritted his teeth, and did what he had to do.

The second he pulled her into his arms, she broke into pieces. Her sobs rocked her narrow shoulders as she wailed into his chest. Her small form curled against him trustingly, and he tightened his hold, muttering nonsensical words against her temple.

Seeing her every day at the store, without Austin as a buffer, had eroded their barrier as good friends. Soon after they'd met, he'd accepted her as an extension of his closest friend, though Cord had seen her first. It'd been easy to see why Austin loved her so much. A part of Cord loved her too. The trick was loving the right amount, something he struggled with, and not only in his relationship with December.

But working together had chipped away some of the barriers he'd painstakingly built. Noticing the extra length of her dark lashes might be reasonable, but being charmed by her slight overbite surely wasn't. He'd been studying her too intently, absorbed by every little quality down to her food preferences. Who put duck sauce on egg rolls? Ember did, and it was a sweet quirk.

The way she tipped her head and gave a person her full attention, dark eyes intent and focused, inferring they were special. Every little idiosyncrasy mesmerized him. Because Ember *liked* other people, she cared, and it showed.

Breathing in the scent of her hair bordered on perverted, because he caught himself doing it every time and did it anyway. It stirred something in him. Fuck. *Stirred something?* That shit was for romance books.

Despite his efforts to minimize the attraction, their current proximity had his body hardening, and she was upset! He needed some distance. This was his best friend's wife. *Wife.* Marriage was serious shit.

Awkwardly, he rocked her a little, willing comfort and trying for safe distance. Her arms slid around his waist, getting closer, and he tried not to breathe into the press of her softness. Her hair was a mess, falling out of her bun thing, and he itched to bury his fingers in the soft strands.

Fuck. This is bad.

How long could girls cry? Cord was sort of a savant when it came to useless knowledge. He knew a pig could orgasm for thirty minutes, a flamingo could only eat with its head upside down, and a snail could sleep for three years. But he didn't have a fucking clue how long a woman could cry like this.

He was suffocating. "Can I get you, like, some water?"

"No. Thanks."

Oh, thank God. Words. Slurred, nearly indecipherable, but words nonetheless.

"How about a pillow? When my mom cries she usually hugs a pillow."

"No, thank you."

"Do you want your tea now?"

"No, thank you."

Give me something! He couldn't stand situations he couldn't fix. "Why don't you take off your boots?"

She nodded weakly, but didn't move. Christ. Tightening his mouth, he leaned forward. Her wilted form clung to him as he removed one boot then the other.

Aww, look at her little feet.

His gaze jerked away before he inspected her toes. "Are you hungry?"

"No."

"I'll be right back." Carefully extricating himself, he wedged a coarse throw pillow—one that came with the couch—within the circle of her arms. He'd probably had his boots on the damn thing...

Retreating to his bedroom, he left the door open only a crack, keeping his eye on her as he dialed. She just sat there staring at nothing as he whispered.

"You motherfucker. Austin, I swear to all that is holy, if you don't get over here and fix this right now, I'm going to beat you senseless next time I see you. She's a fucking mess. I don't know what to do!" Searching his room for any kind of comfort, he yanked a pillow off the bed then tossed it back, exchanging it for a fluffier one. Like pillows were helping, but at least this one didn't have dirt and soup stains on it. He hissed into the phone again, "You're a dead man."

Pocketing the device, he returned to the living room. "I got you a better pillow."

The second he held it within reaching distance her arms choked the life out of it, hugging it close. Every hair on his body stood on end. Something about her actions seemed so desperate, so starved.

Having known Austin his entire life, there was certain information he'd acquired about the man. There was a time he and Austin discussed everything, their hopes, dreams, goals, sex. They didn't talk as much as they used to after he and Ember said their vows, but he supposed when guys got married, their wives sort of talked them out.

But Cord knew Austin was a sexual guy much like himself, though Cord could personally admit he was probably a bit more...intense than his friends realized. Yet December seemed utterly starved of physical contact. He swallowed, locking that observation away, in no rush to awaken old demons.

He and Austin each agreed if they ever settled down, the women would have to be something special. None of that 'I have a headache' bullshit. Their wives would have to possess a healthy sexual appetite, comparable to theirs, in order to qualify as *The One*.

Austin hadn't exactly boasted about his wife's insatiable nature, but he'd alluded to it, seeming wholly satisfied in that department. So why did Ember seem deprived of even the slightest physical comfort?

Cord studied her death grip on his pillow and his chest got heavy, remembering her response the other day when he'd told her she needed to get laid. None of this was right.

Ember was Austin's *One*. She made him complete, made him try harder than he ever wanted to try. Made him see value in himself. What kind of shit had gone down between them to land them here?

Jesus. This was a fucking disaster and he didn't have all the information. He didn't think he could ask December any more personal questions, and his asshole friend wasn't talking to him. He couldn't fix this without knowing stuff. Where was Austin, the great guy he'd grown up with who made this woman—now sobbing on the couch—so happy?

He might not be equipped to deal with the situation, but they were his friends, and if Austin couldn't take responsibility he'd have to stand in for now. With a resigned sigh, he did what he had to do.

"Okay, up you go."

She gasped as he lifted her into his arms. She was so little, like carrying around a doll or something. Kicking open his bedroom door, he carefully deposited her on the bed. It practically swallowed her whole.

After adjusting the pillows and blankets and tucking her in like a child, he went to dig up something for a headache. If her head wasn't pounding yet, it would be soon. It wasn't natural for a person to cry that much.

When he returned with two pills and a glass of water, she hadn't moved an inch. He sat on the edge of the bed.

"Take this for me, kiddo."

She made no move to accept the pills, so he took control.

Slipping his arm under her shoulders, he hoisted her up.

"Open."

Those full pink lips parted and he deposited the capsules behind her bottom teeth.

"Sip." He pressed the glass to her lips and she took a tiny swallow. "Good girl. Drink a little more for me."

It seemed even the task of swallowing two pills and taking a few sips of water was beyond her strength, but she obeyed him. Placing the glass on the nightstand, he eased her back and tucked her under the covers again. Her eyes remained open, the dark irises flecked with gold like vacant windows.

Easing the tendrils of hair free from her wet cheeks, he allowed himself the slightest satisfaction of feeling its softness between his calloused fingers.

"Do you want to take this out?" he asked, giving her bun thing a little nudge. It looked complicated and uncomfortable, and everything inside of him demanded he find an excuse to touch her.

She shrugged. Was that a yes? A no?

He focused on the band twisted around the bun. How the fuck did she get that in there? His fingers gently tried to unravel the puzzle as she rested in silence against the pillows. Would scissors be inappropriate? At least her sobs had diminished to the occasional hiccup and her tears had mostly dried. Finally, he unraveled the hair tie.

Holy crap she had a lot of hair. Now that it was untwisted he wasn't sure what to do with all of it. He didn't recall it ever being this long. Did women sleep with it under their heads or spread over the pillows? He never woke up with any of his dates so he wasn't clear on protocol.

Running his fingers through the dark strands, he carefully untangled all the snarls and knots. Chocolate waves rippled over white cotton sheets as he admired the different brunette hues. Her hair was quickly becoming his favorite color.

Time to go.

He stood. "I'll be in the den if you need anything, kiddo. Just give a shout. There's water and a paper towel here for you...if you need to cry some more. Again."

As he backed out of the room he shut off the main light, but kept the lamp on the dresser lit. He left the door cracked, so he could check on her without disturbing her.

Carrying the untouched tea to the sink, he dumped it and collected the litter of crumpled tissues she'd dragged from her pockets. The idea of December waking up to evidence of her breakdown, and possibly triggering a repeat episode, was terrifying.

Once he had the room straightened up, he reclined on the couch and found the remote. Watching television felt wrong, but he couldn't just hover by the bedroom door. His mind drifted as he flicked through channels, wondering what tomorrow would bring.

He hoped December would be talking more by then. Fortunately, they both had weekends off and his dad had the store covered, his mom helping out. It had always been like that, run by and passed down through each generation, man and wife, side by side. Maybe that's why it felt so right having December there this week. Of course, she wasn't his wife, so it really wasn't the same at all.

As his thoughts drifted to Austin a white-hot rage lit deep inside of him, somewhat mitigated by the uneasy realization there was something really wrong with the man. No way would Austin treat December poorly unless he was in the throes of something out of his league.

If it was the booze, it was a major problem, and one only Austin himself could decide to rectify. Worry hollowed Cord's belly.

The sound of a floorboard squeaking caught his attention. December stood at the edge of the hall watching him. Tossing the remote aside, he levered up on an elbow. She gestured for him to stay still.

"You okay, kiddo? Do you need something?"

She moved closer and perched on the lip of the couch cushion, near his knees. "Can I sit with you?"

Ah, crap.

"Sure." He tried to maneuver into a seated position and give her room but she tipped sideways and tucked herself against him. Spoons. *Jesus.*

Her hair was all over the place, literally in his face, forcing him to breathe her in with each breath. Unsure where to rest his hand, his palm hovered over her hip. He finally gripped the back of the couch to avoid draping his arm over her or pulling her closer.

She wiggled a bit and he stiffened. Once her generous bottom nestled against his pelvis, she sighed and seemed satisfied and he gave up blinking. Her small form relaxed, maybe for the first time tonight.

Alarm bells rang insistently in his head. His body wasn't relaxing. Not at all. Things were transpiring that abso-fucking-lutely should not be happening. Sweat beaded on his brow as he willed the inappropriate awareness to subside—and failed.

"I have to use the bathroom."

He squirmed out from behind her, the couch shifting against his frantic movements. Ember nearly toppled to the floor before grabbing at the cushions to anchor her weight. He bolted down the hall, shutting the bathroom door securely between them. His fingers tugged off his wool cap and fisted in his curly hair.

What. The. Ever-loving. Fuck?

He quickly checked his phone. Nothing.

Pressing his palms into the sink, he faced the mirror and sucked in gulps of air that should've been calming.

Meeting his wild, blue stare in the mirror, he whispered, "Knock it off, pervert. You don't get to think about her that way. Not. Yours. You hear me? Not. Fucking. Yours. Get through the next few hours and tomorrow you get to murder Austin."

Shutting his eyes, he waited for his body to calm. When it did, he flushed the toilet and washed his hands, so she wouldn't think he was in the bathroom talking down his dick.

She was sitting up on the couch when he returned to the den, so he hovered on the edge of the carpet. Exhaustion showed in her tired eyes and listless posture. The girl needed sleep.

"Why don't you go back to bed, December? You look drained. You need rest and the bed's more comfortable."

She nodded, but didn't stand. Watching him, she quietly asked, "Will you lay with me? I'm so tired of sleeping alone."

Whoa!

His panic must have shown, because she quickly said, "Never mind."

God, he felt like a monster. He wasn't rejecting her because there was something wrong with her. She was perfect. It was an ethical issue, a married issue, a, *there's some fucked up emotions resurfacing here* issue.

She pushed to her feet, her efforts deliberate and halting. Tentative steps took her back to his bedroom. Forcing his feet to remain planted in the den, he listened as the fabric rustled and the mattress sighed. Each whispered rasp of fabric upped his inappropriate desire as she settled into *his* bed. Finally, the house quieted.

See? She's fine. She'll fall asleep and everything will be good.

The silence lasted only a minute when a muffled whimper marred it, tearing at his heart. That agonized sound...

"Goddamn it," he growled under his breath.

Snatching up the remote, he killed the TV and went to his room. December lay curled beneath the bed linens, visibly trembling as she tried to contain her pain. He couldn't leave her like that.

Rounding the bed, he climbed onto it, ensuring the covers formed a barrier between them. "Hey. I'm here. It's okay."

She rolled to her side, and stared solemnly. Little red hives splotched the fair skin beneath her spiked lashes. Somehow his fingers found a resting spot at her neck, just beneath her ear, and traveled slowly until they traced along the arch of her cheek.

His thumb glided over her thin brow, combing all the dark hairs in the same direction. He'd never experienced something that felt so right while knowing it was irrefutably wrong.

She watched him silently, blinking only every once in a while. He couldn't begin to describe what he read on her face or in the depths of those brown eyes, but his heart flinched.

"I'm sorry he hurt you," he whispered.

Her lashes lowered and her lips compressed as another sound of distress forced its way up her throat. Crap. He shouldn't have said anything. What the fuck had the asshole actually done? She couldn't, or wouldn't say.

Tears seeped past her lashes, traveling down the curve of her nose and rolling into the little divot above her lips. His touch swiped the drop away. Her lips were so soft against his calloused skin. She was probably wondering if he soaked his hands in battery acid. He quickly withdrew his touch.

Watching a woman cry in silence was like watching a rare white peacock fall for the thrill of the hunt. It shouldn't happen. Such fragile beauty shouldn't suffer. Ever.

"He doesn't deserve your tears."

"This isn't the real him," she murmured, so low he barely caught the words.

"I know it isn't." And he did know.

Her eyes closed. "He never touches me anymore, not even like you're touching me now."

Cord froze, everything inside of him calling attention to how close they were. Lips just a breath apart, eyes focused so intently he could count every lash, name every freckle and tease every trace of peach fuzz by simply breathing. Too close. He shifted back and removed his fingers. How had they ended up here?

"Please don't... Don't pull away."

His eyes closed and he groaned. "December..."

"I know. I just... Do you know what starvation feels like? Not annoying hunger, but the actual pain of starving. It's like my skin is starved for contact. Please. Just hold me a little while."

"This isn't right. You're married and he's my best friend."

She inched backward and chewed her bottom lip. "I know. I shouldn't even ask. I'm so screwed up, Cord. I don't know what I'm doing."

Oh, God, he was hurting her too. "Shh... It's okay. I'll lay with you."

Wide eyes searched his and a bit of relief softened the set of her mouth. He eased back and her body scooted closer, nestling into the nook of his shoulder. Her little hand picked up his wrist, draping it over her hip. Her arms curled in front of her chest as she lay her cheek right over his heart. Could she hear how fast it was beating?

Giving in, he pulled her tighter to him. It was a big brother hug, he told himself, but knew that was a lie. Having his arms around her seemed the only way to ease her pain.

He pressed his lips into her silky hair and whispered, "Try to get some sleep. We'll figure everything out in the morning."

Resting his chin on her head, he thought up ways to punish Austin. Her breathing leveled out as her body relaxed, and she slowly drifted to sleep. He remained tense—and as hard as stone.

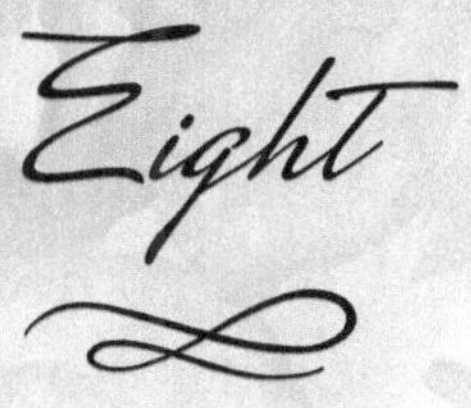

Eight

Cord

CORD AWOKE and stretched out like a starfish before opening his eyes. Something was different. Cracking apart his lids, he searched his room. Everything appeared normal.

He sniffed. Bacon. Fresh wood burning in the fire. And...female.

"Shit."

His gaze darted to where her cup should have been on the nightstand. It was gone, and all his books were neatly stacked. Did she clean? Sitting up, he took inventory of his room and frowned. Where the hell were his piles of clothes? Oh, this was so not good.

Making quick use of the bathroom, he washed up and paced as he called Austin for the hundredth time. His voice remained low, but he ran the water just in case Ember had some crazy bat hearing.

"Yo, asshole. I don't know what the fuck's going on, but you need to come collect your wife. I took care of her last night for you, but that's the last time. Man up and deal with your shit. She doesn't deserve this and you know it." He ground his teeth. "Don't make me come there."

Venturing into the kitchen, he pasted on a smile. "Good morning."

December turned and knocked the wind out of him without even touching him. Her face was clear of all blotchy, crying blemishes. Her eyes were vibrant and her smile enchanting. She wore one of his flannels over her clothes from yesterday and her feet were bundled up in a pair of his hunting socks.

"Good morning. I made breakfast."

Swallowing, he searched for something appropriate to say. "I had stuff to make breakfast?"

Lowering into a chair, he watched her cautiously as she placed a steaming cup of coffee in front of him. Hey, he remembered that mug. It had been missing for months.

"You had some pancake mix and syrup in the

cupboard, but no butter, so you'll have to make do unless you want more tomato soup."

His stomach lurched at the thought. Last count he had seventy-three cans left. Pancakes sounded sensational. "You look like you're feeling better."

"I am. I slept like a rock. I haven't woken up so refreshed in months. While I was looking for food, I noticed an odor coming from your washer. I ran the load you left sitting with some white vinegar to get the musty smell out. It's in the dryer now. I hope you don't mind."

Mind? God, no. He hated doing laundry and anything else domestic. The same uneasy feeling from the bedroom overtook him. "Thanks."

She slid a towering stack of pancakes cozied up to a side of bacon—what man didn't have bacon in the house—in front of him, and some silverware wrapped prettily in a napkin. "Thanks."

"I carried in some wood from out front and piled it by the fireplace since you were running low. I hope that's okay."

"Uh, yeah, thanks." What the fuck was wrong with his friend that he'd mistreat this woman?

She settled in across from him with a much smaller plate of pancakes and unraveled her fork and knife. He stared, mesmerized, as she neatly cut into the fluffy pile drizzled in amber syrup and hummed over the first bite. Her eyes closed in ecstasy. His mind leapt to other things and he reined it in.

"Have you talked to Austin?"

She stilled and he regretted ruining her peaceful morning, but what were they doing? They couldn't play house and pretend this was normal.

She carefully rested her fork on the edge of the plate and folded her hands as she met his gaze. "No."

"What exactly is happening here, Ember? I'm a little confused." It had to be bad, but he needed to hear it.

"Austin's leaving me."

"*What?*" Whatever he expected her to say, it wasn't that. He'd thought she might consider leaving Austin, but for his friend to ditch Ember...the man was insane. "That can't be right."

"He's home now—"

"How do you know?"

"Because I have both sets of keys and he was too drunk to tie his shoes when I left."

"What happened?"

The narrow column of her throat moved as she swallowed. His hands itched to comfort her, but he remained still.

"I'm sick of lying to protect him when he

isn't concerned one bit with protecting me. We haven't shared a bed in ten months. We barely speak to each other and I cry at least once every day. Some days my tears don't stop until I fall asleep and sometimes I wake up because I'm crying *in* my sleep. I'm sick of it."

It was unbelievable. Everything he knew of Austin went against the picture she painted. Austin had always been so intuitive, freakishly sure of his future. He was kind and compassionate and one of the most thoughtful men Cord knew. His mind literally couldn't grasp what she was saying, except he'd been witness to those tears and had no doubt she spoke the truth.

Her tone was level as she went on. "We had a fight when he found out I was working for you and he told me he wanted me to quit. I refused, because we need the money and, well, I like my job. Working is good for me right now. He's being irrational and someone needs to take responsibility. Our recycling bin's overflowing with beer cans and liquor bottles and I can't seem to find him awake and sober long enough to have a real conversation about our decaying relationship."

"I knew he'd take issue with you working at the store." Maybe if he focused on that one thing, he could pretend he hadn't heard the rest.

Although he should have manned up and faced his buddy down himself, instead of leaving it to December, by the sound of things.

"It's not just that. Last night he pulled out old photos and...I don't know what he was trying to do. Seduce me, maybe? I don't know. He reeked of whiskey and got mad when I pulled away. Then he said it was because..."

"Because?"

She shifted and looked away. "He thinks you..."

"I, what?"

"It's stupid."

A lot of Austin's recent behavior was stupid, so he could only guess. "Tell me. I won't take it personally. Is it because I gave you guys money?"

"Yes and no. That's part of it, but he also has the crazy idea that I..." She waved her hand as though searching for words she couldn't find. "*Like* you, I guess."

Shit. *Don't overreact.* "Well, we're friends."

"Austin thinks it's more than that, like we're doing something behind his back. He's totally paranoid."

Was he? Fuck. Cord tamped that shit right down.

His personal feelings shouldn't play into this. They made no difference and never would. Certain lines would never be crossed. And fuck

Austin for thinking him that shitty of a friend. "That's ridiculous. We're friends. That's all."

Of course he loved them, at times maybe a little too much. It was easy to play the martyr, act like the gaps in their interactions were a result of not being invited over, but sometimes a little forced distance could be a huge relief. They were so damn happy, so much so it sometimes made him sad, which essentially made him a terrible person.

He never expected them to hit a rough patch like this. Austin had an impenetrable shell and Ember was *everything* to him. Good shit like that didn't just fall apart, but according to her, the man was breaking. It hurt, that despite their long friendship, he hadn't reached out to Cord either.

December gave him a sad smile. "He told me to get out as if it was only *his* house. I wouldn't leave, so he packed up and prepared to go. I grabbed his keys before he got downstairs. There was no way I was letting him drive like that."

His mind stumbled over Ember ensuring Austin's safety regardless of how he'd treated her. *That* was love and devotion.

"So what happens now?" He hated the caution lacing his tone.

She shrugged. "After I clean up from breakfast I'll go home and talk to him. If he wants me to go, I won't stay. I can't go on being ignored anymore. It's...how I feel defies description. It's beyond agonizing."

"I had no idea things had gotten this bad. I'm so sorry, swee—kiddo." Christ, he'd nearly saddled her with an endearment. *She needs a friend, idiot.*

"There's nothing to apologize for. This morning I woke up and felt like a light bulb finally went off. I've been fighting for him to come back to me and he resists again and again. I believe he loves me. I don't think a love like ours can die. But he hurt me. I won't stand around so he can go off on rampages and binges and keep lashing out at me while destroying himself. If he isn't going to put me first, I have to." Avoiding his stare, she muttered, "And he needs to start taking care of himself again, because he's taken that job out of my hands."

She was incredibly strong. This was a total turnaround from the drippy woman in his house last night. His chest swelled with pride.

"Where will you go?"

He watched as a great deal of her bravado wilted. Ah, there was her Achilles' heel. If she had normal parents she could go home, but December's parents didn't have a house. They drifted from place to place with the stability of a feather in the wind.

"I...I'm not sure. I know this all seems drastic, but it's far from over. I still can't accept that the man I'm dealing with is the same person I married. I refuse to believe he's never coming back to me. My presence isn't helping matters though, so maybe if I remove myself for a while, he'll snap out of it. But I don't know what to do about the house."

Right, because their finances were in the shitter. They could barely afford the home they had. Their circumstances didn't allow for her to rent an apartment.

And, bad judgment rising up, in three, two, one... "You could stay here."

"No. I couldn't put you out like that."

Exactly. "It's fine. Really." Why was he still talking? "It would be nice to have some company for a while."

"Cord, think of what you're offering."

Yeah, stupid. Think!

"I am. We're friends. You could save on gas, because we could carpool to work. You like to cook. I like to eat. You're tidy." He gestured pointedly around his house. "If you can tolerate me leaving a trail like a slug everywhere I go, then I don't see a problem."

She searched his face, the stupid grin curving his lips totally foreign.

"I don't know, Cord. Austin would freak."

"He's lost any say in the matter." Truer

words and all, but he was excruciatingly aware he was taking a side here and changing the dynamics of an ancient friendship.

However, Ember was his friend too, and where else could she go? Live in her car? He couldn't stand to see her suffer any more indignities. Someone needed to protect her. Austin would come to understand that—surely—once he got help and was thinking clearly again.

She released a long breath. "It wouldn't be forever. Just until Austin works out his issues."

Which could take years and wind up in divorce if his friend didn't wise the fuck up.

What are you going to do then, dick? You're volunteering for something way out of your league here, not to mention traipsing over what Austin considers very *private territory. Bad idea.*

So bad, he had no choice but to ensure she and Austin fixed their marriage and everything went back to normal—his little crush a nonexistent, never to be mentioned, blip in the past.

Normal, that was the goal here. Back to normal. Yeah, that was the right attitude. Get involved, save the day, but keep his distance. "I just want to see you guys get through this. Anyway I can help, I'm there for *both* of you." Saying it out loud helped.

"Are you sure?"

No. "Absolutely, one hundred percent positive."

Her smile was soft and slow, as she offered him a look that demolished many of his remaining reservations. "You're such a good friend, Cord."

No, I'm not.

He sobered as he considered his decision might not even matter once she talked to Austin. The guy could apologize and the drama would dissipate. Cord's intervention wouldn't be necessary and Ember wouldn't need to live in his house. With him. As a friend.

Their reconciliation was paramount. So why did he suddenly feel so cheated by the prospect of his offer being an unnecessary one?

Nine

Austin

AUSTIN SAT on the steps facing the front door and grinding his molars into little nubs. Where the hell was she? His phone was lost on silent somewhere—probably dead. His fucking keys were also missing—both sets.

He'd torn the house apart in a rage last night, and when he woke up this morning, worried sick about his missing wife, everything was a blur. The throbbing in his head wasn't helping matters. So he sat, praying the blank spots of his mind would somehow fill in.

Wheels crunched over the snow and he shot to his feet, flinging open the door. Ember

167

climbed out and navigated her way through the snow. Relief shot through him as soon as he set eyes on her.

Shit. He needed to shovel the walk. "Be careful."

She stilled, noticing him for the first time. "You're awake."

"Where were you?"

She carefully took the steps without answering. He stepped aside as she entered the house. He waited for an explanation as she removed her hat and coat. When she faced him he saw red.

"Whose shirt is that?"

She looked down and flushed, her eyes wide as they returned to his. "Let's go to the kitchen and talk."

She spent the night somewhere else—with someone else—and now she's wearing his clothes.

He grabbed the sleeve of the flannel and thwarted her escape. "Answer the fucking question, Ember." The sight of her in another man's shirt tightened his chest with indescribable pain as his mind reeled with debilitating panic.

Yanking her arm back, she snapped, "Stop talking to me like that. I'll answer you once we're sitting and you're talking to me like a rational person."

His jaw locked as she marched into the other room. She was wearing another man's shirt! Of course he followed, fuming jealousy mingled with dread.

Yanking out a kitchen chair, he dropped onto the seat. "Talk."

December rolled her eyes and pressed her lips together.

She had some nerve, strolling in here at nine o'clock in the morning, wearing some other man's clothes. He dismissed his fear. Austin Garret did not do fear.

So why are you so fucking terrified?

She folded her hands on the table, the larger sleeves, swallowing her arms. "We need to discuss your drinking."

Give me strength... "Jesus Christ, Ember."

Tension knotted his shoulders as he noted her disgust and glanced away. She never used to look at him like that. He missed the admiration he'd once found in her eyes.

The clear revulsion he glimpsed now destroyed him, brutally gutted him every time he caught the slightest flash of disappointment. He was losing her. Maybe he already had.

Anger seethed at the injustice. He was going through some shit. She was his wife. She wasn't supposed to give up on him, but he doubted so much lately, he couldn't fault her for not wanting to stick around. Still, it fucking pissed him off, because it fucking hurt. Vaguely, he knew he was being selfish, but couldn't find a more noble emotion to replace it.

He waved a hand, falling back on bravado. "Come on. Let's hear it. Tell me all the things I do wrong."

"Could you stop playing the martyr and talk to me for once?"

"I am talking. This is how we talk. You tell me all the ways I disappoint you and I agree to try harder."

I will. I swear. Please don't give up on me. God, he hated himself.

"Austin, stop! You aren't helping."

"When do I ever? I just make your life more difficult. I know. I'm an awful husband. You don't even have to say anything. You're right. You're *always* right." He couldn't muzzle himself, couldn't quit the excuses or undeserved jabs.

"You know why that is?" His beautiful wife didn't wait for an answer. "Because I make the right decisions while you continue to make poor choices. Do you have any idea what it's like to watch you destroy yourself, day in and day out, for months? I can't take it anymore! And whenever I say something to you out of concern, you fly off the handle or drown your sorrows in a bottle. This isn't healthy."

She was making it sound worse than it was, but if it were as simple as not drinking, he'd quit.

Case closed. Between her and booze there wasn't a choice. She won every time. "I'll stop drinking."

She stilled. "You will?"

"Yeah. If that'll make you happy, I'll stop. I love you."

His quick compromise seemed to throw her off, which was pretty insulting. It was one thing to doubt him, but to doubt how much he loved her... That really hurt. With that matter resolved, he got to the real issue.

"Now, tell me whose shirt that is so I know who to kill."

Her eyes narrowed. "Do you even remember last night?"

Not really. "You came home. We had a fight. And you left."

But it was more. She'd been upset, was still upset. He recalled her crying and had a hard time even picturing the memory of anguish twisting her face, not because of blank spots but because it was too agonizing to visualize.

Yeah, he definitely couldn't drink like that anymore.

"I left because you told me to leave and when I refused to go, you said you were leaving. You were drunk and I couldn't let you drive, so I took your keys and left."

He didn't recall any of that, only a lot of

yelling and being really pissed. The vague memory of her distraught, pleading... But what she'd been pleading for remained unclear.

He fucking hated not having all the facts. Quitting drinking for a while probably wasn't a bad idea. He needed to get his head clear. "Where did you go?"

"That's all you're worried about, where I went? Not the things you said or how you hurt me?"

What about what *she* said? Didn't it take two to fight? He wouldn't just flip out, not without some level of provocation. He wasn't an irrational person. He was in the wrong, but it didn't feel like this was totally his fault.

Fuck his fucking piecemealed memory of something that happened less than twelve hours ago! It was beyond frustrating to forget important details, especially those that clearly hurt his wife.

Voice calm, he argued the only truth he had. "I get hurt too, December. Do you think you're the only one capable of feeling pain?"

Even if he couldn't remember what she'd said exactly, he'd been hurting and her words had twisted the blade in the gaping wound that refused to heal. And when he tried to kiss her she rejected him. Yes, he remembered *that*. Never in their relationship had she ever told him no. The second she turned away from him, all sorts of assumptions ran rampant in his head.

Cord. They'd been talking about Cord. "Are you having an affair?"

"*What?*" Her shoulders drew back, her palms flattening on the table as more revulsion flashed in her eyes. "How could you even ask me something like that?"

"A simple 'no' would be nice to hear."

Just say it. No… Please…

"How could you ask that?" she repeated.

Why was she deflecting with another question? Paranoia churned, stirring up his nausea and anger until it was almost impossible to speak. "Are. You. Having. An. Affair?"

Her eyes blinked rapidly as terror choked him.

Say no. Just say no and I'll fix everything.

His gaze traveled over the flannel shirt and fire burned in his gut. If someone else put their hands on her… "Answer the fucking question!"

She flinched as he shouted and tears glazed her eyes, slipping over her soft lashes. He hadn't meant to snap like that. Jesus. Why couldn't she just answer and quit pushing? The sense that too much was happening outside of his control choked him. What the fuck was happening to him?

"No," she rasped, posture stiff and frightened. "I haven't been with anyone in ten months."

Her denial should have relieved him, but it didn't. Nothing seemed to alleviate this rabid paranoia infecting him. It was like a toxic cancer he couldn't escape. And fuck it, if he didn't hear her subtle accusation. "Then whose shirt are you wearing?"

"Cord's."

Or maybe his instincts were spot on. *"Goddamn it!"*

He shoved away from the table and paced, his hand gripping the back of his neck as he struggled to get a bead on reality. "Are you fucking him?"

"Jesus, Austin! Are you unable to hear? I'm not sleeping with anyone! That's part of the problem! Even my husband won't fuck me!"

He pivoted and glared at her, a metaphorical fist slamming into his stomach and nearly dropping him to his knees. What the hell was she talking about? They fucked. They made love. They had uncountable intimate moments—off the charts, going at it like rabbits, ringing both their bells, wild sex. The kind of intense intimacy they both needed.

His mind scrambled for their most recent sexual encounter, but he couldn't fucking think while she was sitting there dressed in another man's clothes. "Take off his shirt."

She hesitated a moment, then her trembling fingers undid the buttons and the shirt slid off her shoulders. She sat in a threadbare thermal. He wanted to snatch the flannel from her and tear it into a thousand shreds then burn every scrap. It was bad enough she and Cord were working together and the guy knew too much of their personal business. Now she was wearing his fucking clothes.

Cord never got under his skin like this, and he didn't like feeling threatened by someone previously trusted. It was unclear who was encouraging what. Was Ember asking him for advice on whatever they did in private, or was Cord butting in where he didn't belong? Either way, boundaries were being crossed. He wasn't putting up with it and he wasn't going to let Ember blame her cozying-up to his best friend on booze.

"I guess you ran off to his place last night. Cord, your shining knight, always there to rescue you from your horrible life here on Happy Fucking Lane."

"Will you stop blaming Cord for everything? Our problems have nothing to do with him! You told me to get out and I left. Where else could I go, Austin? We don't have any money. I couldn't let you leave after drinking half a bottle of Jack. You should be grateful we have a friend like that to take me in when I had nowhere to go in below freezing weather."

That's where that whiskey went. He'd wasted an hour looking for it this morning. And sure this wasn't only about Cord, but he wasn't making things easier. Cord had always been on *his* side. When did that change? Fuck, when did he and Ember get on opposite sides?

Trying not to take refuge in anger, he forced himself to calm. But the truth was, he was angry. There was so much rage burning inside of him he didn't know what to do with it, where it was stemming from, or where to direct it. He grasped it wasn't her fault but she was here and he found himself wanting to dump everything on her.

"You didn't have to go to him," he said slowly.

"Where should I have gone? You didn't care where I went last night. I moved here, because you promised to always take care of me. I gave up my friends, family, all so we could live here, and last night you would have thrown me out like trash." Her trembling fingers dashed away the moisture beneath her eyes and she gulped. "I'm...I'm your *wife*."

Did she think he didn't know that? The pain was back. He desperately wanted to stop with the talking and take her in his arms, make this all go away, and put everything back to the way it always was, but he didn't know how.

The sight of her tears gutted him, made him feel like the most worthless man in the world. She didn't deserve this and yet, he couldn't seem to break through the barrier separating them of late.

"And I'm your husband."

His heart was splitting in two and she rolled her shimmering eyes and chuckled. Fucking laughed. All his vulnerabilities spewed forth and he snapped, "What kind of wife spends the night with her husband's best friend?"

"The abandoned kind!" Her tears seemed to dry instantly as she put aside any show of weakness and glared at him, her words echoing in the silence.

It was too much. He couldn't take full responsibility for landing them in this place. She'd changed too. Everything was different when he only wanted things to stay the way they always were. "Is that what I did? Abandoned you?"

"You never even talk to me anymore. I love you and you completely ignore me. I feel like I have the plague. You won't even touch me."

"Last night I tried to kiss you—"

"You were drunk! It was like making out with a whiskey barrel—"

"I said I'd stop drinking!" Goddamn it, she was pushing him, assuming he'd fail before he even had the chance to try!

"Then do it! Don't just say it, do it! I'm so tired of you saying you'll do something and then nothing happens. You came to bed the other night and you were back on the couch before morning. You throw me scraps and I'm supposed to be grateful and make do? When does it end, Austin? How much am I expected to endure before I reach my limit? I gave up everything for you—"

"Stop saying that as if I made you do something you didn't want to do! You liked our life."

She did. He was sure of it. She told him that all the time. He'd never make her do anything she didn't want to do. Ever. And as far as the other night... He didn't have an explanation.

"Well, I don't like our life anymore."

He drew back, his thoughts derailing, his anger spent. Her words were like a crack to the skull as his rationalizations crumbled. His body sank like dead weight into the chair, legs too numb to keep his balance. Soul sucking silence wove around them, unending and excruciating. How had it come to this?

He couldn't take any more. The wind left his sails as he sat, depleted and limp, totally exhausted with this unending misery neither of them asked for. He was so damn...tired.

"I don't wanna fight," he whispered, dejected.

Her lashes lowered, the weight of too many burdens—burdens he created—forming lines of tension around her eyes and mouth. "I love you, Austin."

Her hand traveled the slight distance to his, but then drew back to the safety of her lap. So much distance. Every exchange stretched them, emotionally and physically, to the point of agony. Yet he couldn't breach the void any more than she could.

This was no way to keep a marriage, together yet so far apart. "Give me your hand."

Watching her hesitate, he caught her fingers in his own. If only she knew, the rage he sometimes let slip was ravaging him every waking second of every day. It wasn't about her. The problem was him. He could never hate her. He hated himself and he just wanted all the anger to go away.

"We can beat this, Ember. We're strong."

Her grip tightened in his and relief tunneled through him, siphoning his strength like water down a drain yet cleaning away the decay so he could pick himself up again.

His body shook as he stared at their locked

fists, holding on to everything that seemed to be slipping through their fingers. It was clear neither of them wanted an outcome that landed them apart, but with the passing of time their marriage had somehow become so fragile, so brittle. He wasn't sure how to handle it any more —at least not without causing further damage.

They'd fallen into such a dark abyss neither of them could find a simple way out. It was *his* job to protect them, to lead them. He'd failed her and he had to get right with himself if he ever expected to get right with her again. Because a life without December...

He couldn't even think it.

"No more fighting, Ember."

"I don't want to fight either, but it seems that's the only way we communicate anymore."

Blowing out a breath, he gathered his courage. "I'm sorry for everything—all of it. This isn't me."

"I know it's not, Austin. That's why I'm so scared. I see us falling apart and I want to pull you back before you're any further away, but you lash out and—"

"I don't know why." Truth be told, he was scared too—terrified. "I'll be better. I know you don't believe me, but...just trust me one more time. We'll find our way back to where we were. I'll get us out of this."

Her lashes lowered and her mouth tightened. Pain was evident in her expression and he suffered it, knowing he'd caused it. How was it even a debate to give him another chance? Ember always believed in him. That she couldn't put the same blind faith in him she once had...it crucified him.

He needed her to give him another chance. She was hurt and rightly so. There was no excuse for his neglect, and most confusing of all, he didn't even have an explanation to justify it to himself. He loved her more than anything or anyone else in this world. None of this made sense.

If it was the drinking, then he'd quit. It didn't matter that a shot right now would ease his anxiety and help the words flow better. He'd sacrifice anything to save them, because without them, there was no point to anything. He needed her, needed her to trust him again.

Attempting to regain her trust, he forced out the apology that hurt both of them to hear. "I'm sorry about the...sex. I want to fix it. I want to fix us. I love you, December."

Wrapping his other hand over their fisted ones, he whispered, "You're my life, my soul. I don't know how everything got so fucked up, but I know it can get better." *It has to.*

She sniffled, but he was too much of a

coward to look at her. He had nearly destroyed what they had and he didn't want to risk completing that deadly task. Everything in his life had always revolved around impeccable self-control. He'd fallen in love with December, fallen for everything about her. And when he'd asked her to marry him, it was because he wanted to give her a better life than anyone else ever could.

The day she said yes had been the greatest day of his entire life. To hear she no longer liked their life...it was an excruciating wake up call.

His chest tightened as the threat of losing everything they had resonated. In only a few split seconds their past flashed before his eyes, peppered with glimpses of a future he'd yet to see.

They used to make love in the mornings. And while he showered, she'd slip into the kitchen to make coffee. He cherished her, not because she obliged him, but because she took care of him and let him take care of her too. And soon, together, they were supposed to be taking care of a family. It was simply unfathomable to think that might not happen now.

To think he'd pushed away this woman... Her unconditional love had made him the richest man in the world and he deeply cherished her. To know he'd cut her down to this...

His apology was ragged, raw with shame.

"I'm so sorry I let things get so out of control." It wasn't enough.

"I'm sorry too." Her quiet words slashed deep.

"Don't apologize. I'm the one who did this to us."

"Life happens, Austin. It's how we deal with it that matters."

And he hadn't been dealing, unable to accept the loss of his career, bitter because his loyalty and dedication to the company hadn't even garnered severance pay. And the jobs out there... One job that was offered didn't cover their expenses and the next was without benefits. Or the hours were insane, especially if they decided to have a child.

He held out, held on—yet he hadn't held *up* his end of the bargain. December had somehow been making ends meet and he'd been hiding in a bottle.

Cord had offered work, but Austin's pride quashed that opportunity. His best friend was a great guy, but it felt too much like charity. Maybe keeping Cord at bay helped him delude himself further. Admitting they needed Cord's help would be admitting, once and for all, Cord was the better man. And if that was true, how the fuck could he ever justify being the one to win December?

He stared at his beautiful wife. Her face still tight with tension but her eyes soft with love for him as she met his gaze. His chest constricted even as his heart tried to beat its way out. "Do you remember the first thing I said to you?"

Her lips formed a tremulous smile. "You said, 'You're gonna be my wife.'"

He smirked at the familiarity of it. There had never been a time he was more certain about anything. "I was right."

"You usually are." Her matter-of-fact statement came with such confidence it jolted him, restored a smidgen of his lost faith in his dependability. That's what she always did—believed in him—so much so that she taught him it was okay to have faith in himself.

"I've been wrong about a lot of things lately, Ember." It wasn't as hard to admit as he thought, probably because it was true.

Her smile faded. "What are you saying?"

"I never wanted to treat my wife the way I've treated you over the past few months. Things *are* going to change. We'll get back on our feet, back to the way we were."

Her lips pursed. "Maybe backward isn't the way we should be going, Austin. Life throws curveballs. This one may be the first, but it certainly won't be the last."

"No, I know I can fix this. I just need to believe in myself again and I need to know you believe in me. You have no idea how much I depend on your faith. I'll get a job and I'll quit drinking. I'll sleep in our bed again. I *want* to sleep in our bed again."

Her eyes blinked rapidly. "I'd like that."

"Come here."

Her slight hesitation killed, but he had only himself to blame. Slowly, she rose from her chair and stepped in front of him. He laced his fingers through hers and pulled her to his lap where she fit perfectly.

She turned her face into his shoulder and he kissed the soft spot beneath her ear. "I love you, Ember. I promise it won't be like this anymore."

Her shaky breath carved a permanent hole in his heart, one he'd feel forever as a reminder of why change was necessary.

"I love you too, Austin."

The softness of her body against his, the way her personal scent tantalized his senses... He tightened the circle of his arms. December was right where she belonged. Relief that he'd dodged a bullet of his own making made him light headed. Tender relief and possessive need awoke his physical desire.

Rising with her snuggled close, pushing past the effects of the booze he'd consumed to dull his hurt pride, he strode to the den, blessing whatever intuition had insisted he gather up and dispose of the worst of his excess. Lowering his wife to the couch, he reveled in the way she stared up at him, trust sparking in the depths of her dark eyes.

Anticipation lit her beautiful features and he knew everything would be all right. December was the only drug he needed. So long as he held onto her, the world would right itself.

Dropping to one knee, he skimmed a hand over her hair, following the thick strands to where they streamed across her shoulders. The thin shirt she wore did little to conceal the lace bra—or confine the swell of her breasts. He traced those tender curves, relishing her tiny gasp.

"May I?" His diffidence registered, not his typical approach, but after so much time lost, he wasn't sure he had the right.

Her lips pressed together before lifting in a smile. "I want you, Austin. That's never changed. You never asked before..."

She was right. Asking was never his practice, but his confidence was sketchy at best at the moment. He tried to center himself, knowing Ember preferred him taking up the aggressive role, got off on it as much as he did from fulfilling it.

There was an unfamiliar awkwardness to

unveiling her body and he tried to slow down, to savor the moment. His body was so hard he ached, and he prayed that his cock wouldn't betray him and soften, drowning in the tide of alcohol that streamed in his veins. When she reached for him, slipping a hand under the waistband of his pants, he gritted his teeth so as not to disgrace himself. This time was for her.

"No, baby." Threading his fingers through her much smaller ones, he raised her hand above her head, pressing it into the cushion. He urged the other to join it, gratified at her compliance.

Easing off her jeans, along with her white panties, her arousal perfumed the air. If ever a man could rejoice at such a scent, he was that guy. Leaning in, he pressed a kiss against her belly then nipped along her hipbone.

Her thighs parted, the tender inner flesh a beacon and he nuzzled there, breathing in her scent and softness. He groaned and licked along the crease where her hip led to her pelvis, his tongue dancing to whisper over the smooth skin of her pussy.

Moisture slicked that sweet flesh, a taste he'd know anywhere, and he sought its source. She shifted restlessly, and he levered one of her legs over his shoulder, opening her to him.

"Austin, please..."

He rose to the occasion, slipping a hand beneath her buttocks to lift her to his mouth, his eager tongue investigating every tiny crevice, pressing deep into her channel before searching out the tiny knot of nerves at the top of her sex. He worked circles with his tongue, suckling and teasing as she writhed and chanted his name.

Her breathy cries built in crescendo as he edged her higher until her muscles tightened under his touch and she softly shuddered with release.

His free hand reached to caress her breast, then pinched the taut nipple through her shirt as he drew out the last vestiges of her orgasm. She panted quietly as he laid a gentle, open-mouthed kiss on her swollen pussy.

Removing his jeans, he crawled over her. Her arms wreathed around him, pulling him close as he guided himself into her clenching sex. His prayers answered, his erection didn't flag, perhaps inspired by the adrenaline of averting that impending loss. His hips worked of their own volition, as he focused on the face of his beautiful wife, her eyes slightly dazed with satisfied desire.

He gave up his control, his limbs trembling as she drew forth his release faster than he would have liked. Now, more than ever, his need for her had been affirmed and her acceptance of his love cemented his commitment to do better, to be the man she deserved, the man he once was and desperately wanted to be again. He would fix everything for her—he had to, because losing her was not an option.

As his body sagged to rest within the circle of her embrace, his demons momentarily laid to rest, her shoulders trembled and he sensed her surge of emotion. Unable to face her, reluctant to own the pain he'd certainly caused, he internally crucified himself for all the mistakes he'd made, for which she'd paid the price.

No more. He would be the man he'd always been.

Pulling her into his hold, willing his soul-deep affection for this woman to calm her fears, he made a silent vow that he would not lose control again. It was a big promise, one he'd made before, but this time he meant it.

Rather than cause further pain with oft-repeated vows, he said only what he knew she'd accept as truth. "I love you."

As they lay in the shelter of each other's arms, Austin sensed reality beating on the door. Staying there forever wouldn't erase the road ahead any more than sex could shorten the distance they had to go. December was the first to acknowledge the creeping restlessness as she shifted back on the pillows and their connection was broken.

"You okay?" he quietly asked as she reached for her discarded clothes.

Her glance skittered to his face and she blushed a soft shade of pink. "I'm better."

He smiled nervously. "That was...nice." Reaching for her fingers, he gave them a soft squeeze. "I've missed us."

"Me too."

Silence became a physical mass between them, uncomfortable to bear and draining. Despite all he could say, he kept quiet, too afraid he might awaken a demon in the quiet.

"I should clean up," she muttered, her face partially hidden behind her hair.

"Yeah. Okay."

Her smile was tentative as she glanced at the hall and back to him. She leaned down and brushed her lips across his. His fingers curled around her wrist, holding her there as something inside of him feared letting her go. This wasn't perfect, but it was more right than it had been in a long time.

"I love you, Ember."

Her smile seemed more sincere than it had a moment ago. "I love you too."

He let her go and watched as she walked away, hoping she'd come back still smiling. The sudden pressure to do something else nice for her arose, and he searched his mind for ways to keep her smiling.

He had dinner started by the time she wandered into the kitchen, the picture of a well-fucked woman. Her gorgeous hair fell in tangles around her sex-softened face, and she blinked at him from eyes as sweet as chocolate.

His chest swelled with satisfaction, but he took even greater pride in the fact that he'd cobbled together a meal from the measly contents of their pantry. He might not have been pulling his weight around here, and he'd be happy to get back into the provider role, he owed her as much.

"You're cooking?" Her eyes lit with slight humor. There was a time he'd had to support himself. Though he wasn't anything close to the incredible cook she'd proven to be, he managed not to starve.

Covering the flush heating the back of his neck, he bit his lip and grinned. "It's nothin' fancy."

Her nose lifted as she sniffed the air. "It smells good."

"It's just a boxed casserole you had in the cabinet. I found tuna in the pantry."

Her smile compensated for the twinge of unease he suffered at their role reversal. Not that taking care of his wife in this manner was somehow beneath him, he just sucked at it. She always managed to make even the easiest meal special and beautiful. He struggled to find a decent pan. He needed to prove he could do better. Little attempts like this would make that point.

"Have a seat." He shuffled her to her chair where he'd set out a plate.

"I'm starved."

"No doubt. Working girl and all." As soon as the words left his mouth he winced. The last thing they needed was a repeat argument.

Her forehead creased. "Austin..."

"Hey. No, it's good. You did what you had to do, and I get it."

He did get it, but that didn't mean he was giving up on getting back to the way things were. This was temporary and he'd suffer the setback until he got his shit in order, which needed to be fucking soon.

Resting a hand on hers, he softly promised, "We'll get back to the way things were when I find work. It'll be soon, Ember."

"Right." She hopped up and went to the cabinets, lifting down two glasses.

He didn't want to interpret her reply as uncertainty, so he shoved away *his* insecurities and tried to present a decent meal. It would have helped if they had some sort of side dish, but that was no one's fault but his. They really needed to get some money.

Naturally, December seemed a touch anxious, sitting back while he fumbled his way through preparing dinner. The kitchen was definitely her domain, but he wanted to do something thoughtful for a change.

"Can I help?"

"You just relax. It should be done in a minute."

He took every opportunity to touch her and was gratified when she leaned into him by the slightest degree. God, he missed her.

The timer beeped and he opened the oven, fanning away the steam. As he rummaged around for a potholder, she smirked and mumbled, "The drawer next to the sink."

"Thanks."

The casserole looked nothing like the ones Ember could make, but it wasn't burnt so that was a plus. He pulled it out and set it on the stove as he grabbed the napkins off the counter. Reaching for the pan, he singed his finger and jerked back. "Ah, shit!"

"You okay?"

He reeled in his temper and gritted his teeth. "Yeah." He grabbed the potholder and cautiously carried the dish to the table. "Careful. It's hot."

She plated their food and passed him his serving. He'd give anything to be eating something she prepared, but it was what it was.

"This is good." She forked up another bite.

No, it wasn't. "I have a limited menu. Maybe tomorrow I'll attempt breakfast."

Her sweet smile brightened the whole kitchen and his cheeks stretched as he returned it. Things were going to be just fine so long as he kept earning smiles like that.

Fuck. What the hell was he going to make for breakfast? He needed a job soon, because this domestic stuff was way outside of his wheelhouse.

Clearing his throat, he tried for what once was normal conversation. "So how was your week?"

He caught the hesitation in her eyes and sensed before she answered that this was awkward for her too. Damn.

"It was good."

Trying not to mention Cord, he treaded lightly. "What do you do there?"

"Mostly work at the register and help customers. I'm studying the kitchen inventory and Cord thinks I'm a natural saleswoman."

His molars clenched, but he forced what he hoped was a passable smile. "Good."

It wasn't good. It was misleading, sending her in a direction far away from the road they'd been on.

Reminding himself—and her—that this was temporary, he said, "Hopefully I'll get a call soon and we can go back to normal."

Once again a look of doubt flashed in her eyes, but she covered it well. "I heard there might be some new construction once the snow clears."

That was months away. He needed something sooner or they'd get stuck in this twisted routine and never find their way out. He made a noncommittal sound and finished his plate.

The silence stretched to a near stifling thrum that prickled his nerves. She rose to clear the table and he intercepted. "I'll get that."

She hesitated and he took her plate, shutting his eyes and drawing in a patient breath as he faced the sink. "I'll do the dishes," he offered. "Why don't you take a soak in the tub?"

"Are...are you sure?"

God, he could barely breathe. "Yeah. You worked all week. Go relax. I'll handle the cleanup."

She backed out of the kitchen and he nearly collapsed with relief when he was alone again. It wasn't that he disliked spending time with her.

He loved her. She was his favorite person. But he was so high-strung and freaked out he might somehow screw something up he was more comfortable alone.

Little by little, he told himself. Little by little they'd find their way back to normal.

Dishes weren't his favorite task, but he'd do anything to repair the damage and this seemed like a fast step in the right direction. As he scrubbed and rinsed, his thoughts strayed to the bottle he'd stashed in the living room beneath the DVD rack. His mouth pursed—merely for swallow to wash away the taste of that casserole.

With a scowl, he scrubbed the rag over the table, and then the counter, resisting the urge to hurl the inoffensive material into the sink. He had to keep his hands moving so the shaking was less evident. God, he was ready to fucking snap and he didn't understand why.

Once the kitchen was clean he anxiously sought out a new distraction but came up short. He'd told Ember he was done with drinking, and he was.

Fuck!

He grabbed his coat and forced himself to leave the house just to prove he wouldn't let her down. The steps and walk needed shoveling before morning, and the cold air would clear his head.

As he inserted the shovel into the layers of ice and snow, he worked up a sweat and hopefully purged some of the toxins at the same time. As he labored it became evident how out of practice his muscles were. Every corner he turned seemed to present another overwhelming dilemma, but he'd build back his stamina and be the man he was meant to be.

Little by little, he'd prove to her he could succeed.

With a lighter step, he made his way back up the porch steps. Once in the house he called up to Ember. "I shoveled the walk."

"Really? Thank you!" Her pleased response wafted to him and he flinched. She shouldn't feel surprised that he'd taken the initiative. All the more reason to keep moving in this direction.

His resolve firmed as he removed his coat and chafed his hands, his gaze drifting to the DVD shelf.

Throw it away.

Dropping to a knee, he untied his boots and left them by the door. Tomorrow he'd clear out all the bottles after she left for work. Did she work tomorrow? Christ, it was bad when he needed a calendar to clarify what day it was. Regardless, he'd wait until she left to get rid of his stash. If she saw him holding one now she'd get the wrong idea and be pissed. Better to wait and let the dust settle.

Mind made up, he shut off the light and took the steps to their bedroom, hoping this was yet another symbolic move to get his life—their lives—back on track.

Ten

December

THE GLASS SHATTERED as he kicked the mirror. "Tell me another! What else do I do wrong?"

December held the folded laundry protectively to her chest and tried to remain calm in the face of this particular storm. "Stop screaming at me."

He stomped across the room and she hustled backward. "I told you not to accept any more money from him!"

She glanced at his splinted hand. Two knuckles had cost a lot of money to fix, especially when they could only afford mediocre medical insurance with astronomical deductibles. "What was I supposed to do, Austin? You need your hands. No one told you to punch that wall."

And now he looked ready to punch another one. He mumbled something she couldn't make out.

"What?"

"We could have paid the bill later."

"And let it accumulate interest?" It was hard enough asking Cord for another loan on top of the one they already had, not to mention hiding the reason they needed the money, which she'd done out of respect for Austin's privacy. She shouldn't have to justify yet another solution to a problem he brought on himself. "We're already in a hole."

"Then stop borrowing money!"

"If you don't want to lose our home, we have to. Why don't you get that? My paycheck isn't enough to afford more than our mortgage and groceries. We have other expenses. You need a phone in case someone calls about a job. You need a car to get to that job. You need insurance to drive that car. And you need functional hands to work."

"Well, that ain't happening now!"

She angrily stuffed the laundry into the drawer and crouched down to clean up the broken shards of glass. God only knew how long it would take to replace the mirror.

"Leave it," he snapped.

"I'm not going to leave shattered pieces of glass all over the bedroom floor."

Here they were again, him drunk and her astounded that he'd broken yet another promise. Such a fast return to hell only two weeks after their reconnection. No job and he was drinking again. Still. How gullible was she? She couldn't continue to hide behind how much she loved him—a love that was rapidly corroding with hate.

"I said leave it, before you cut yourself."

As if his words were the catalyst, she hissed as a thin shard sliced into the pad of her thumb.

"God damn it, Ember! I fucking told you to leave it alone."

Staring down at the swelling line of blood collecting on her finger, she fell back onto her ass, stunned. Yet again, it all came down to her screwing up, being the outlet Austin required to avoid his own accountability.

Defining moments should be accompanied by a sound like a crack of thunder clapping loud enough to rock a person's world. But in actuality, silence denoted such moments, as the pivotal point settled with utter clarity in the mind.

She placed the collection of glass back on the

floor and stood, cupping her hand so blood didn't drip on the carpet.

"Is it bad?" he asked, as she made her way to the bathroom.

Too late for concern, Austin. Hollow and meaningless.

His drinking had worsened after a brief respite. The wonderful man she'd married had drowned beneath alcohol and murky lies. Each sense of abandonment had hurt more than the previous one, but this time as he pulled back, she barely registered the pain.

She ignored him and focused on meticulously cleaning out the gash. The old Austin would have jumped into action the second she was injured. Taken charge. This timid man observing from a safe distance was not her husband. But then the old Austin never would have acted out.

He'd become a petty tyrant in their own home, breaking the beautiful things inside, just as he was breaking her. She was not immune to the reach of his destruction.

She saw through the anger to the fear, and pitied him, but it was time to face the truth. People, no doubt, would think her a slow learner, and perhaps she was, except she couldn't throw away a great marriage and an even greater husband without doing everything possible to recover them. But her efforts weren't enough. *She* wasn't enough, and that awareness further numbed the pain and paved her path.

As the water cleansed the cut, running pink with her blood, she mentally organized her belongings. She'd need clothes for work, toiletries, her checkbook, the laptop in order to pay their bills.

Some other clothes. Her vitamins. Austin would need to come up with half the mortgage. She'd pay for her half until they made a decision about what to do with the house. Strangely aware of the next step and all it signified, she hadn't anticipated the calmness that cocooned her once the decision was made.

It was truly time to go.

She'd pay for her car insurance and half of the phone bill. He may not have a job now, but he'd have to get one if he wanted to keep their house. And if not...

So be it. Carrying him on her shoulders wasn't doing either of them any favors.

Once the blood slowed, she wrapped her finger tightly with gauze and taped it with the supplies in the medicine cabinet. With a bottle dangling from his fingers, Austin stepped away from the doorway so she could pass.

"Are you okay? Do you need stitches?"

She glanced at his free hand, bandaged up much like hers. Weren't they a pair?

"I need a lot of things, Austin, and I haven't been okay for a while." Her voice was so level and quiet it surprised her. Where had such stability come from? She sounded nothing like herself.

She'd suffered enough shouting and arguing to last a lifetime. Not looking forward to another fight, she made her way through the rest of the house, gathering up her belongings. As she carried the first load to the car, her computer and the wedding picture that had graced their hall table, Austin was nowhere to be found.

Sucking in a breath, she prepared for a confrontation. There was no way leaving would be easy. She took the steps and retrieved the suitcase from the hall closet. Austin was sitting on the chair in their bedroom when she returned to pack.

"Going somewhere?"

Without making eye contact, she focused on emptying her drawers. "I'm leaving. I'll come back when you're sober and proven you can stay that way."

The nearly empty bottle dropped to the carpet with a muffled thud. "There. I stopped. Now stay."

She shook her head and stacked her t-shirts

in the upper left corner of the suitcase. "It's going to take more than that. You've promised to quit before. Lots of times. I think it's time we admit your drinking's become a problem you can't control on your own. You need help, Austin."

"You're my wife. *You're* supposed to help me."

Pulling in a long breath, she prayed for patience. "I've tried. I think you're severely depressed and drinking makes it worse. I can't fix this for you. You have to do it for yourself."

"So you're leaving? Just like that?" Funny how his words were slurred yet slashed just the same.

"I've tried talking to you. You see reason for a heartbeat—just enough to make me believe I'm enough, but then you go back on your word and we both lose. I'm not the motivation you need. I'm not sure I'm anything to you anymore." And why were they doing this dance again? Why was she arguing with a drunk? This was the continuous drain of energy she needed to escape.

"You're everything. When did I ever say you weren't enough, Ember?"

"I'm not enough to make you stop drinking. You have to do this for yourself."

"What about in sickness and in health? I

guess that was just some bullshit promise to you."

"What about love and honor, Austin? Protect? You mope around here, breaking our home and hurting yourself—hurting me. You aren't loving or honoring either of us by acting that way." *And I can't obey you anymore.*

"I'm sick. You think I don't know there's something wrong with me? I know it. I swear, this time I'll stop drinking for good. Look." He carried the bottle to the bathroom and poured the remaining drops down the toilet and flushed. "Gone. I'll empty all of them."

"And then you'll waste money on more. We've been through this before."

"Stop being so fucking cold."

And now came the nastiness. Looking him dead in the eye, she gave him the truth. "You made me that way."

The bottle shattered in the tub and she jumped. "God damn it, Ember! You're not fucking leaving me. This is *our* house! You're *my* wife."

With trembling fingers, she quickly zipped the luggage, her calm slipping. She could get the rest later. Keeping close to the perimeter of the room, she made her way to the door. His footsteps hammered across the floor.

With one foot in the hallway, the suitcase was ripped from her hands. "I said no!"

"You don't have a choice!" she shouted, pushed past her limit. "I'm leaving and you're scaring me! Now, stop it!"

"You're not fucking leaving." His eyes were wild as he held onto the bag. She couldn't do this. Cutting her losses, she bolted down the stairs and grabbed her coat and keys.

"December!"

Covering her ears with her palms, she quickly got behind the wheel and slammed the door to the Jeep, cutting off his screams. Her hands trembled so fiercely she dropped the keys and had to blindly fish them out from under the seat.

Austin burst through the front door just as her fingers closed around the serrated metal. She jabbed the keys into the ignition, turning over the engine with a squeal.

He shouted and barreled down the steps, his voice filtering through the glass and over the sound of the motor. "I need you!"

What about what I need?

Slamming her foot on the gas, she gunned it down the drive. Her tires spun when she reached the road and it blurred behind her tears. The pain, the pain was back and it was unbearable.

She needed to get away and then she'd pull over and make the call.

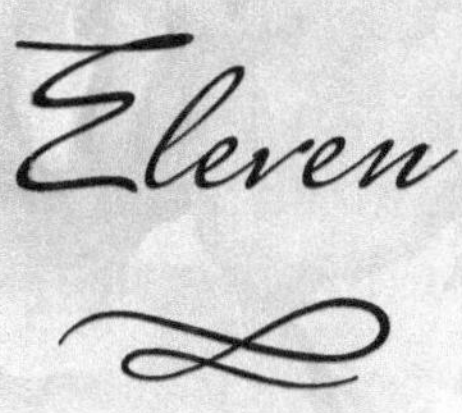

Cord

CORD'S PHONE rattled against the loose change in the cup holder, rasping out the lyrics from *Hide Your Love Away*. Recognizing the ringtone, he smiled and lifted the phone out of the console.

"Hey, little lady. How's it shaking?" There was an uneven sigh on the other end. His foot eased off the gas. "December?"

"Cord..."

"What's wrong? Are you hurt?"

"I left."

Fuck. "Where are you now?"

"I'm down the street from my house." Her

words were choppy, yet resigned. "He...wouldn't let me leave. He has my bag. I...I...couldn't fight with him anymore. So I left it."

Motherfucker. He pulled a fast U-turn and headed toward their place. "Did he..."

Jesus, he knew he shouldn't have let her stay there when she told him Austin had started drinking again.

He focused on the facts, pushing his feelings back until they got things squared away. "Are you okay?"

"He didn't hurt me. At least not physically."

Okay. She was okay. But he didn't like that empty tone in her voice. "Stay put. I'm only a few minutes away. I'll be there soon. Don't drive and lock the car doors. Call me back if he shows up."

He raced through traffic and shouted at every dumbass driver in his way. Austin hadn't returned any of his calls and, out of respect for Ember, he'd given the couple space. Again. She'd hinted at reconciliation, but Cord was skeptical. Still, when she asked him to cut Austin some slack, he'd reluctantly agreed—against his better judgment.

After running at least two yellowish-red lights, he finally spotted December's Jeep pulled onto the shoulder of the road. He parked on the other side of the street and jogged over to her window. Her arms were slouched over the wheel, her face hidden under her hair. When he knocked on the glass she jumped. Damn it, she looked like hell, so freaking pale and her big eyes rimmed with red.

Her shoulder lifted as she rolled down the window. The movement was awkward as if she were in some sort of physical pain. He'd fucking murder Austin if he'd laid a hand on her.

Her face contorted for a moment before she gained control. Then he saw her hand, a thick bandage enveloping a finger. "What the fuck happened?"

"He broke a mirror and I cut myself cleaning it up."

Someone was going to die. Smothering a growl, he calmly gave her instructions, having noted that she did well with being succinctly told what to do when emotions were high. "I'm going to go get your things. I want you to stay here until I come back. Then we'll take my truck to my place and come get your Jeep later. Don't open the door for anyone. Do you understand?"

She nodded, and he leaned in and kissed her forehead. "Put the heat on. It's cold."

He returned to his truck and drove to Austin's. The door was unlocked so he didn't bother knocking. "Austin!"

The punch came out of nowhere, knocking

Cord into the wall. It got his attention, but Austin was too drunk to aim properly. Finding his bearings, Cord turned and showed him how a proper punch should be administered, relishing the opportunity.

Austin stumbled into the dining room and crashed into the furniture, sprawling out on top of the table. But Cord wasn't through.

"Get up."

"Fuck you," Austin growled, licking at the ruby split on his lip.

Cord stared, furious, but that niggle of fear unfurled deeper in his belly. Was he losing his friend? A shiver licked up his spine before he got a grip. No matter his feelings on the issue, December was huddled in her vehicle down the road, a fucking mess. And the man in front of him—the one he once admired and loved—was responsible.

"Fuck *me*? How about fuck *you*, Austin? Do you have any idea what you've done? You had *everything* and this is how you act after she gave you another chance?"

Shaking his head, Cord turned toward the stairs. "I'm getting her things. Don't bother her until you have your shit together."

The second Cord's foot touched the first step Austin let out an ungodly roar and tackled him. Cord cursed as he was dragged to the ground. Drunk or not, Austin was a strong son of a bitch.

Punches jackhammered into his side as he struggled to roll on top of Austin and restrain him. When he wouldn't back off, Cord landed an uppercut that shut him down quick.

"*What the hell is wrong with you?*" he barked, shoving Austin's dead weight off of him. He stood and brushed at his clothes. "Sober the fuck up!"

Marching up the stairs, he spied a suitcase lying sideways in the hall. He grabbed it and made his way back downstairs where Austin was still muttering on the floor.

"She's *my* wife," he growled.

Cord stilled. Shaking his head, he towered over Austin. "And her husband's a great guy. Why don't you find him so all this bullshit can stop?"

"If you were my friend you'd stay out of it." The mumbled rejoinder was astonishingly clear, considering Austin's state.

Cord dropped the suitcase on the porch before turning to grab Austin by the collar of his shirt, hoisting him to his knees and demanding his full attention.

"Try to get this through your liquor drenched skull so you remember it when you're sober. If I *wasn't* your friend, I'd stay out of it.

Bailing you out of bankruptcy, holding your wife while she cried, giving her a job and some goddamn dignity back, I did all of that because I fucking *love* you."

His heart pinched at the truth he'd never dared to utter, and he sucked in a massive breath. "Me taking your wife in so she has a safe place to sleep... I'm doing that because she's my friend, too, and no one treats my friends the way you have."

With an extra shake for good measure he dropped him to the ground and stomped to his car. He was glad to find December where he left her. Pulling up behind her Jeep, he exited his truck and went to her door.

Giving the glass two quick raps, he nodded in greeting. "Open up, kiddo. I got your things."

She searched his face before unlocking the door, her motions painfully sluggish, as if everything was still sinking in. Reaching over her, he removed the keys from the ignition. "You need anything out of here before tomorrow?"

"My computer's in the back." She slowly slid out of the driver's seat, and he grabbed her laptop.

Checking to see everything was secure, he walked her to the passenger side of the truck and held the door as she climbed in. "Buckle up."

He didn't take her straight to his house. Instead, he went to the town market. "You wanna come in or wait here? I just need to pick up a few things."

"I'll wait here if you don't mind."

That was probably best, but he didn't like leaving her. Her movements and her words were hesitant as though she wasn't tracking well.

"I shouldn't be long."

Thirty long minutes and two hundred dollars later he was pushing a cart full of things he'd never purchased before in his life. Rumors about his personal habits were probably already circulating.

He'd grabbed anything he found that was stereotypically female. Fruity soaps, detergents, scented candles, Midol, quilted toilet paper with little cherubs printed on the packaging—fuck the utilitarian stuff at his store—several pints of ice cream, the most expensive chocolates, tampons, anything that said Summer's Eve, vegetables he didn't know how to pronounce, cheeses that came from goats and other strange animals. Chicken breasts, salad mixed from strange leaves. And steaks for him.

Somehow he still felt unprepared. There would be lots of girl tears and there was no way to get over his fear of such things. He needed to be proactive and do everything possible to keep her together while Austin sobered up and fixed their marriage.

Once he had everything loaded in the bed of the truck, he returned to the cab. "How you holding up?"

"You were gone for a long time. I hope you didn't go out of your way on my account, Cord. You've already done enough."

Thank God she's talking. "Of course not. Just had to pick up my usual items."

"The truck's filled with tomato soup, isn't it?"

He laughed. She was making jokes? That was unexpected and a huge fucking relief. "No, I actually bought some real food this week."

When he pulled up at his house, he again gave her specific instructions.

"I want you to go inside and pick out a set of sheets from the linen closet. I'll unload everything and while you're taking stuff out of the grocery bags, I'll make up the guest room for you since your hand's banged up."

The sight of her bandaged hand—telltale red stains advertising the depth of the cut—really pissed him off and made him want to hit Austin all over again. Harder. But it was important he keep her moving so she didn't stop long enough to fall apart.

"Okay."

Once he had everything unloaded, she was already in the kitchen folding up bags, the contents on the counter. "Where do you want me to put your copy of *Vogue* and *Women's Day*?"

Heat rushed to his face. "Uh..." She'd get mad if he told her he got those magazines for her, but why the hell else would he buy them? "Okay, you got me. I grabbed them for you."

Her head tilted. "Aw, you don't have to lie, Cord. It's okay. I always assumed you were in touch with your feminine side. I'll just put them in your room next to your aromatherapy candles. And the douche."

As she turned toward his room she wore a smirk on her lips. She was acting so normal. He decided to roll with it. "Hey, I'm all man!"

Her laughter rang through the hall. "Whatever you say. It wouldn't matter anyhow. I don't judge."

"I *love* vaginas!"

She returned to the kitchen. "Obviously. I have to imagine with all the feminine hygiene products you own, yours is in impeccable shape."

"December."

"Cord." Her lips twitched as they had a staring contest.

He let out a breath. "Fine. I got you a bunch of shit at the store, but I don't want to hear anything about it. You're my guest and I wanted to make you feel at home."

"Cordovan! I told you not to buy me anything."

"Girls need stuff I don't have here!"

"You think I need two hundred tampons?" She shook her head and waved a big package at him. "And what about these?"

He shrugged. "I wasn't really being selective. I've never been in that aisle before."

"These are *Depends*! They're diapers for old people! I'm not incontinent!"

"How was I supposed to know? There was a picture of a flower on the front and they were next to all the girlie stuff."

She tossed diapers at him and he quickly stashed them in a cabinet. Every time he saw the bandage on her hand he was tempted to examine the wound, but didn't want to ruin her pleasant mood. How the hell was she so...together at a time like this?

He watched her silently for a few minutes, mesmerized by her femininity and strange behavior. She looked good in his kitchen. "I got steaks for tonight."

"I saw." She opened the lower cabinets and rooted around in them.

"Are you looking for something?"

She sniffled, yet her actions spoke of calm collectiveness. "Where's your cutting board?"

"I just use the table."

She sniffled again. Was she crying? Fuck. No. There was to be no crying! They were joking and talking about his ladylike shopping list and love of vaginas. No tears should be happening.

Sniffle. Her back was toward him as she cut up produce on a plate. How did women know what to do with all that stuff? And that plate was going to dull his knife.

"I was going to make a salad, if that's okay with you." Sniffle.

Shit. Didn't women get whiplash from shifting emotional gears so fast? Stepping close, he hesitated a moment then rested his hand on her shoulder. "We can talk about it if you need to."

Her head shook as she continued to cut vegetables into neat little rows. "No." Sniffle. "I don't want to." Sniffle. "I've had enough for today. I just want to enjoy a peaceful meal and not think about my problems for a little while." Sniffle. "Can you hand me a tissue?"

He turned and frantically searched for tissues. "Shit. I forgot tissues." He ran to the bathroom and wadded up a bunch of toilet paper. "Here."

She took it and quickly wiped her eyes and nose.

His toes bounced in his boots and he fought back the urge to make the most uncomfortable sound a man could produce, the garbled syllable lodging deep in his throat. Why did women have to cry? And they were fine with it, just dripping away. Did they enjoy crying? "Can I help with anything?"

Maybe he should run out and buy a carton of tissues, give her time to dry up.

"No, I'll take care of dinner. Why don't you go relax? Do what you'd usually do if I wasn't here."

Take off my pants and drink a beer in the living room?

"I'm gonna go check on some stuff outside."

He grabbed his coat and fled. Maybe when he returned her eyes wouldn't be leaking anymore. He felt so helpless when she cried, and he loathed identifying with any sort of helpless role. He was a doer, a fixer. Damn tears.

Ember was always complaining she was chilly, so he decided to move some wood from the back to the porch. He'd keep the fire going for her.

Twelve

December

THE TABLE WAS SET and dinner was ready. Cord still wasn't back yet, so December put on her coat and boots and went to find him. The wind bit through her jeans the second she stepped outside. It was nights like this that truly defined bitter cold.

"Cord?"

"Right here."

She twisted and found him stacking wood in the log rack. "Dinner's—where's your coat?" He was only wearing his thermal shirt.

"I got hot stacking the wood. Dinner ready?"

Was he insane? "Are you crazy? It's two degrees out. You'll get sick."

He grinned and grabbed the sling filled with some choice pieces of split wood. "I'll be fine. Come on. Let's eat." He held the door and she stepped back into the warmth.

Her body shivered, her core temperature dropping from standing out there for a mere minute. Cord was sweating. "There's something wrong with you."

He laughed. "Why?"

"You need a coat in this weather. That's how you catch pneumonia."

"That's a myth. Pneumonia's a bacterial infection in the lungs. The cold can aggravate the immune system's normal response, but the bacterium has to already exist in order for the cold to cause an active infection."

She stared, knowing her mouth had dropped open. "A simple 'that's not true' would've worked."

His mouth kicked up in a half smirk. "It's not as much fun as making an inarguable point and seeing that look on your face."

"Whatever. Wash your hands. They're probably loaded with *bacteria*." She carried the dishes to the table and they settled in.

"Would it bother you if I have a beer?"

"No. Just don't go punching walls and kicking mirrors."

He laughed. It was a nervous reflex, she understood. "Sorry. That wasn't funny."

"No, it's not. But I kind of have to laugh about it too, so I don't cry."

"Laughter is definitely better than tears."

"Do you have anything other than beer to drink?" She hadn't had alcohol in so long. It was as if she thought her abstaining could somehow influence Austin.

"Sure. I have wine. Want me to open a bottle? I'll join you."

"Wine sounds great."

"Red or white? I have no idea how to match liquor to food."

"Um...red."

Cord found a bottle opener—no easy task in his kitchen—and poured them each a portion. When he held up his glass, she mimicked his salute and he smiled. "Happy Valentine's Day."

Wine filled her mouth and she froze. Forcing the swallow of earthy liquid down her throat, she rasped, "What?"

"It's February fourteenth. I thought you knew."

"No." A collage of loving images from past years with Austin replayed in her mind at light speed, soured by the events of the day. She swallowed again, her throat suddenly dry. "He didn't even get me a card." She'd picked his out last week. It was probably still sitting in the hutch.

It was stupid to worry about silly Hallmark cards and chocolates in light of everything else, but for some reason this additional slight was so profound it spun everything right into perspective.

"I'm sorry. I shouldn't have said anything." Cord's big hand tightened around the cup of wine he held and she made herself look in his eyes and laugh.

"No. It's not your fault. Wow." She chugged her wine and returned the cup to the table with a click. "May I please have some more?"

He refilled her cup. He didn't have stemmed glasses, but this cup was working out just fine. She needed more than a small serving at the moment.

He glanced at his plate. "Should we eat? It looks delicious."

"What? Oh, yes. Help yourself."

She sat back in her chair, arms crossed over her chest, cup of wine parked right at her lips as thoughts drifted lighter than air through her clouded mind. It was all just fluff. Frosting hiding a shitty cupcake.

"Ember? You gonna eat?"

"Hmm? Oh, yeah. Sorry." She was being rude. Placing her wine on the table she cut into her steak and picked at her salad, not really tasting any of it.

"This is unbelievable. How did you get the meat so flavorful?"

"I marinated it."

He ate like he was ravenous. Austin used to eat like that. It always made cooking so much more rewarding. But over the past month his appetite had changed—all his appetites.

"When?"

Distracted again, she asked, "What?"

"The meat. When did you marinate it?"

"It only takes twenty minutes to marinate beef."

"Delicious," he mumbled through a mouthful. "I grill, but even then it's not like this."

She smiled politely, but her mind was elsewhere. "Do you think he still loves me?"

He stilled. "Uhh..."

"Sorry. I'm like Debbie Downer, aren't I? Enjoy your steak. Forget what I said."

He shook his head.

Was that a *no*? Oh, God, she was going to be sick.

"December, Austin *loves* you. I mean, *really* loves you. You're everything to him. He may not be acting like himself or making the best choices, but I have no doubt he loves you with every fiber of his being. He's frustrated with his behavior, too. It's inexcusable, but never doubt his love for you. What he feels for you...it's as real as it gets."

Her laugh came out cold and resentful. "I would've agreed with you a few months ago, but lately... How does someone change so much? I don't know him anymore. The Austin I fell in love with is just...gone."

"He's not gone. He's in there, fighting to come back to you. Sometimes we get lost and need to combat some demons before we can find our way home. People use distance as a defense mechanism. Trust me. When we can't face what's inside of us, we try to hide it, from others and ourselves. Him pushing you away is his best way of protecting you right now. I have to believe that."

She shook her head, puzzling over his fervent explanation. Trust him? She couldn't focus, her thoughts on her husband and their current predicament. "I wish Austin realized how good of a friend you are to him."

"He's confused right now. Everyone's his enemy, including himself. Once he gets his priorities back in order he'll come around."

"God, I wish I had your faith. I feel like I've

spent all of mine and had it thrown back in my face too much over the past year."

He pushed away his plate and folded his hands on the table, giving her his undivided attention. "Was it really that bad at home? You don't have to tell me anything you don't want to. I'm just trying to understand. If I'm sticking my nose in, tell me to shut up."

Reaching over the salad she snatched the bottle and refilled her cup. "More wine?"

"Sure."

She topped him off. "We've had sex once since May. Two weeks ago when I went home from here and he promised to quit drinking and take a job."

Cord stilled.

"TMI?"

He guzzled his wine. When he finished his glass, he stood and went to the fridge and cracked open a beer. "No, we can talk about this. Has he seen a doctor?"

"I don't think it has to do with his health. I don't know. Maybe he should. I think it's the drinking."

"Alcohol can definitely affect the little soldier in battle."

"That may be true. He sleeps all day then drinks all night. There are only fleeting moments when he's awake and sober. And he blacks out when he drinks hard liquor. It's like he's losing time, but I'm still living at normal speed."

"He's definitely losing something." The somber note in his voice grated against her nerves. Reality was a jagged little pill to swallow at times. Sugar coating it didn't make it any easier.

She stared into her wine, searching for meaning in the ruby depths. "Doesn't he miss me?"

"He's an idiot. Listen, I know this seems like the unsolvable equation right now, but something will get through to him. Tomorrow he'll wake up and realize you're gone. That has to knock some sense into him. Once he realizes what he's lost, he'll put everything he has into getting you back and making this right again. You tell him he has to go to meetings and prove he's done with the booze. He'll do it, December. I know he will."

She needed his optimism, because she was fresh out. The past two weeks started out so hopeful, with Austin actively looking for work and helping out because she was working at the hardware store. But he'd started drinking again within days.

Reaching across the table, she squeezed Cord's hand. "Thank you for believing in him."

They finished the meal in silence, and despite

her angst, there was an unspoken query in the back of her mind. Why was Cord alone on Valentine's Day?

After dinner, December took her time with the dishes, the warm water soothing to her injured hand. Cord hovered for a while, probably concerned with her mental state, until she chased him off to go watch television so she could clean up. She missed feeling needed and appreciated. This shot of domesticity, no matter how make believe, helped her greatly.

Being raised by essentially absent parents definitely made a girl crave a sense of belonging, a sense of purpose. Her parents favored the hippie lifestyle and towed her along without a care to her emotional attachments. Or worse, left her for indefinite periods of time with strangers.

December longed for stability in her life for as long as she could remember, hoping desperately that one day her parents would settle in one place and she might learn the definition of home. That day with them never came, but because of Austin she did learn what home felt like.

His once unshakable reliability, his strong guidance, the voice he gave her in decisions around the house, and her belonging in one place long enough to actually leave an imprint in every room was an incredible gift. If not for him, she never would have believed such a life possible. His drastic withdrawal stole so much of that from her and cast her back into an emotionally frightened past.

"What're you thinking about?"

She startled, and a dish slipped back into the soapy water. Cord relaxed against the fridge, watching her.

Shrugging one shoulder, she smiled. "Thinking about my youth."

"Youth," he scoffed. "You're still a baby."

"And you're an old man, I suppose?"

"Older than you, anyhow."

She rinsed the dish and set it in the strainer. "Do you remember when we first met?"

He smirked, a nostalgic glint in his eye as he nodded. "At that Summer Hops Festival. You were dressed like a hippie and dancing like a wild woman."

"I was a hot mess." *And a little stoned—a lot stoned.*

He crossed the room and grabbed up a towel. "You looked fine. Austin thought so. We both did."

"You were both so...confident. Authoritative, like two alphas in a pride."

Wiping a plate, he studied her. "We were full of ourselves. I guess we knew where we were going in life and figured the world was ours for the taking."

"Austin told me he was going to marry me."

"I remember. Before you even dated or he met your family. That's Austin. He knew what he wanted. You can't help but love him."

When she'd introduced Austin to Rona and Misha, her mother was more taken with his name than the actual man. She told December that *Austin* implied a man of greatness and magnificence. It always irked her that Rona, a guru in nameology, had named her after the darkest month of the year.

"It was like he saw the future." She dunked her hands in and out of the water, chasing a large soap bubble. "I fell in love with him right away." *Too fast.*

No one had ever desired her to that degree. Being wanted was nice, but it was his view of the world that won her heart fair and square. Her mind went back to that first night when they escaped the crowds of the festival and he'd bought her an ice cream cone as her buzz wore off. They'd been sitting on a fence under a draping willow tree, as music played in the distance. Her feet, after having danced barefoot for over an hour, were grass stained and green.

"It looks so charming from here," she said, watching the people as they walked along the fields as vendors peddled craft goods and beer.

Austin's gaze weighed on her and she was

drawn into his attentive stare the same as when he'd walked up to her and bluntly told her she was going to be his wife. She'd laughed, but something deep inside told her his words hinted at truth.

"There's something timeless about the people once you cross the Mason Dixon line," he said.

She crinkled her nose. "It doesn't matter where you are. It matters who you're with."

His head cocked to the side, a half smirk curling his lips as he studied her. "What do you mean by that?"

She shrugged. "I've lived in so many places, and north, south, east, or west, people are people. It takes a special kind of person to actually make you feel at home."

"And what kind of person is that?" His eyes were so intent, providing the answer before she even considered what it might be.

"Home is a place you can depend on."

"Where's your home?" he whispered, seeming to ease closer without moving at all.

"I don't know. I've been trying to find it for the past eighteen years."

"Tell me how you picture it, Ember."

Her cheeks flushed as he shortened her name. It felt significant, as if it implied they shared a bond and therefore could share secrets.

"Did you ever watch the old black and white TV shows? That's how I picture home, but more *colorful. There's something so engaging about seeing a mother care for her family and set the table for supper. It's a dependability I've never known. It seems like such a rewarding role, I can't understand why women shy away from it."*

"Defined."

"What?"

"It's defined," he repeated. "Straightforward. There's no guessing. The husband's the head of the household and the wife's the heartbeat of the home."

Her lashes lifted as she looked into his eyes. There was no sense of mockery in his tone, but rather a feeling of absolute comprehension. "Yes."

"I've always wanted that," he confessed. "I think it would be incredibly rewarding to live that way. Not a lot of women want that though."

"I do," she rasped, never before sharing that side of her dreams with another soul.

His smile was slow and telling. Desire seemed to ricochet between them in that still moment.

"Maybe that's why we're sitting here right now, why I saw you in a crowd of hundreds and couldn't look away. Something about you is different, Ember, and I want to know what it is, if it's what I hope it is, what I've been looking for."

He'd explained the simplicity of family from his viewpoint so eloquently and similar to her fantasies, she was convinced he'd someday have that life. Austin didn't want to live in a constant debate over who held the title of head of the household. He'd wanted the job and she'd wanted to give it to him.

"Ember?"

"Hmm?" She detoured out of memory lane. Cord had dried all the dishes and was staring at her, one eyebrow lifted. "Sorry, I was thinking."

"I said you fell in love with him, but he was ass over heels for you. And I know it. Austin never felt what he feels for you for anyone else. He didn't do relationships before you came along. Always planned to settle once he found the 'one', but had this strange idea she'd stumble into his life when the time was right. Figures, he was right. You two shared so many of the same views. You were...perfect. He'd never let you slip through his fingers."

There always seemed a touch of sadness in Cord's voice when he spoke of that time. Maybe it was losing a bit of his best friend to marriage, a natural occurrence in life. Or maybe it was a touch of envy being that, years later, he still hadn't found his soulmate, considering he held the same values as her and Austin. Regardless, this wasn't the first time she sensed his despondency.

Cord knew better than anyone, all the things that made her fall in love with Austin in the first place. It was as if he couldn't blame her for loving him, because the real Austin was *that* easy to love. And on some level, Cord loved him too. But loving Austin made it all the more painful to oppose him, especially when it was clear that he was hurting. The last thing either of them wanted was to hurt him more.

"I know he loves me," she admitted.

Austin could never let her go before, so it was likely killing him that she was gone now. But the old Austin wouldn't want her to stay in that environment a moment longer and she believed Cord truly understood that.

She dried her hands. "I can handle a challenge, but this has become more than that. We're damaging something precious that's already too banged up."

Cord nodded. "You don't want to see it destroyed."

"Exactly. You know how Austin and I were. There was no power struggle in our marriage. I kept hearth and home and he provided for us. It worked. Maybe it was crazy to define our roles so clearly, to put so much responsibility on one person. I don't know."

"It's how you both wanted it. How *I* would want...a marriage. Austin and I totally understand a stay at home wife's job isn't easy. And I know you appreciated how hard he worked."

"I know you understand. I loved the conciseness of my role. It challenged and satisfied me. Our marriage was drama free—until recently. We had everything. Absolute devotion, genuine affection, and of course love. Intimacy."

He cleared his throat and glanced away. "Yeah. Being in the same room with you two was like taking a bath in…intimacy."

Because what they had was more than sexual compatibility. Intimacy was a part of every interaction from a glance across the room to the passionate moments they shared making love—something they used to do quite often. Austin got her, understood what she needed…

She blushed. "I thought we had it all. That we were perfect." *My, how things have changed.*

"Your marriage was the poster child, Ember. At least I thought so."

She watched him for a moment, again noting all the ways he reminded her of Austin. "I haven't given up hope." But her tired soul needed a break from the pain.

The frightening part was that her husband's thoughts, words and actions weren't aligning anymore. Telling her to leave, refusing to let her go. And once he stopped hiding behind alcohol… What if he sincerely needed her to leave and get out of his life? That would truly destroy her.

Her heart ached with longing for Austin.

Missed him on a spiritual level. The physical absence came second, although it was complimentary. She wanted him back and feared she might never have him again. She loved him too much to force him to stay in a marriage that made him miserable. If he'd heal without her, she'd give him his freedom. The bone deep terror of being without him overwhelmed her, but she'd do it— if that was what he needed to be well again.

"You all right, kiddo?"

She blinked at Cord, lost in her thoughts again. She couldn't share her deepest fear. "Yeah."

"That doesn't sound too convincing."

Trying for a smile and failing, she confessed, "My head's wandering to places it probably shouldn't. I think I'm going to take a shower and unpack."

He nodded. "Okay. Towels are in the closet down the hall. They're not folded, but they're clean."

December organized her clothes in the old dresser in the spare room and carried her towel and pajamas to the bathroom. As she undressed and started the shower, letting the water warm, she cursed, realizing she forgot her conditioner in her suitcase.

Wrapping her body in the towel, she headed back to the guestroom. As she rounded the corner of the hallway she smacked right into the wall of Cord's chest. Strong hands closed around her bare shoulders, steadying her, and the air sucked out of her lungs.

They each stared at one another, doing a little dance in the small space, seeking the right of way. Cord laughed nervously. "You go left. I'll go right." He laughed again when they each moved in the same direction.

"Your right's my left," she said, flushing to the hem of the towel.

"Right. We'll both go *right*."

Finally making it past him, she ducked into her room, heart racing. Awkward didn't describe that moment. There was something wrong with her.

Rummaging through her bag, she tsked when she realized she hadn't packed the conditioner. Strange how such an insignificant oversight could rupture her calm so completely. It was no reason to cry, but her throat tightened and—

She jumped when Cord knocked at the door. "Ember?"

"Yes?" Her voice shook, and she cautiously sent a glance in his direction, working hard to get her emotions under control.

"Do you always leave the water running?"

"I...forgot something. I haven't showered yet."

"Oh." He studied her for a moment and she sensed his concern.

She looked around the room, her surroundings still a bit unfamiliar. Trying to diffuse his worry, she shoved down her frustration and said, "I forgot my conditioner."

He nodded. "We can grab some tomorrow." With a strange blankness to his face, he left her alone.

She stepped into the hall and froze in place. Cord was still standing there. Their eyes met. He appeared almost in pain.

Her hands tightened the fold of her towel. "Are you okay?"

His head shook slowly, his gaze never leaving hers. "No."

"What's the matter?" Her heart rate was not only too fast, but also slightly erratic.

His glance drifted to the wall and back to her. "This."

She gasped as he took a quick step forward and slammed his mouth down on hers. He was *kissing* her. Cord—*Austin's best friend*—was kissing her. Her chest nearly exploded as the hammering behind her ribs tripled in speed and pressure.

His lips were firm over hers, his tongue soft as it pressed into her mouth. She hadn't been kissed like that in so long. She forgot how a talented press of firm lips could rattle her senses. His fingers slid up the back of her neck and threaded through her hair, holding her steady as her mind scrambled to deny the pleasure of having a man's mouth on her again.

Flashing back to that dream, she abruptly regained her senses, his touch striking too close to home. Ripping her mouth from his, she gasped. *"What are you doing?"*

He sucked his bottom lip between his teeth as his eyes, stormy and troubled, stared into hers. "I...I don't know."

Turning, he swiped his wool cap off his head, turbulent curls springing forth. "Fuck!" He pivoted again, this time his face tight with worry. "That never happened. Okay? It *never* happened. It's my fault. I'm sorry. I'm a fucking asshole. *Fuck!*"

She flinched as he shouted.

He apologized again. "Sorry. The last thing you need is another guy yelling at you. I'm just really pissed off at myself right now. I had no right to do that. I'm usually way better at controlling myself than that."

She blinked, thoroughly confused, while he paced in the narrow hall and muttered apology after apology. She knew she was desperate for affection, but what was *his* excuse?

"*Why* did you do it, Cord?"

He turned and paused, as though thinking of an answer. "I...don't know. I wanted to. But I didn't realize I wanted to until I did it and it was already happening."

"Why?"

His head tipped back as he eyed the ceiling. "Because I'm an idiot. I don't know. Maybe because I can't stop worrying about if you're all right and fearing you might cry again. Maybe because it's Valentine's Day and someone should kiss you. Maybe because you're pretty and always smell good. And you look fantastic in that towel. Maybe because I think about you when you aren't around, and how wonderful you are. Or maybe because I'm just fucked up."

"You're not fucked up."

"Oh, I'm pretty sure I am."

"Cord—"

"You're *married*, Ember! You're married to my *best friend*."

She nodded, seeing his evident distress over the situation but unsure how to comfort it. Why wasn't *she* more upset?

She cast about for guilt but hit a brick wall. It was like the married part of her had been cut off from communicating with her brain, all common sense amputated. Most troubling, she sort of wanted him to kiss her again.

Her face tingled and she was sure she was flushed. Trying to make light of it in order to ease his upset, she lamely joked, "You're a good kisser."

"Please don't say shit like that, December."

She laughed, her mind preoccupied with the absolute present and completely disinterested in the bigger picture. Maybe she was having some sort of manic episode or a breakdown. "Why? It's true. I don't think I've been kissed like that in over a year."

He paced some more. "See. It's shit like that that pisses me off. How could he not kiss you like that every single day? You're fucking gorgeous and sweet and so easy to talk to—"

"You think I'm gorgeous?" Her neglected heart grabbed hold of his words.

He shot her a disapproving look. "A blind man would find you beautiful. There's something about you...But that doesn't matter. You have a husband and he's not me. I'm sorry I kissed you."

"I'm not."

Huh. She hadn't really thought that through, but she wasn't one bit sorry. There was no regret. No guilt. A glimpse of pleasure that promised much more. A tiny bit of sympathy for

Cord existed, because he clearly felt terrible about it, but as far as it impacting her marriage and Austin...nothing. Maybe if the man she'd married was waiting at home, but there was only a stranger living there.

"I'll leave you alone." He turned and she rushed after him, catching him by the back of his shirt.

"Wait."

He stilled, but didn't face her. His broad shoulders lifted with each labored breath and she felt a chill run down his back as if the weight of her fingers released something dark buried deep in his soul. Taking slow steps, so not to spook him, she moved around his towering form. His breathing was unsteady and his eyes were closed.

"Look at me." Giving orders wasn't who she was, but she needed to see inside him.

His lashes slowly lifted, revealing a turbulent storm in his eyes. "Ember..."

"Shh..." Lifting onto her toes, her heart thundered in her chest, the broken pieces of her heart forgotten for a short span of time as she focused on all that was peaceful and momentarily forgot the pain.

Rising the last inch, she closed the distance between them and brushed her lips across his mouth without lingering too long. Deep satisfaction bloomed inside of her, a healing balm that bore intangible forgiveness for wrongs that could never be undone.

"Thank you," she whispered, her breath mingling with his. "Happy Valentine's Day."

As she lowered to the soles of her feet she glanced away, catching a glimpse of balled fists at his side. He didn't say a word as she returned to the bathroom.

Thirteen

Cord

THE BATHROOM DOOR closed and Cord stood, his feet nailed to the floor, body a tense wreck, staring at the space she'd vacated. This was bad. Bad. Bad. Bad.

"Fuck."

He looked at his watch. It was almost nine at night. He wanted to take off and build some space. A whole lot of space. Maybe he should. He could go get her car, but then how would he get his truck home? He'd moved wood, gone to the store. There was really no excuse to leave again.

What the hell would he do when Austin

found out? He'd never done anything to betray his friend before and didn't understand how he could act so thoughtlessly now. It was like his brain was on vacation.

He could say he was thinking with his dick, but that wasn't right either. He hadn't kissed her on some extreme jolt of lust, although he couldn't deny she tied him in knots. He'd kissed her out of necessity—the sudden, insane, inexplicable need to ease his heart. And hers.

December's situation sucked more than he was prepared to comprehend. It was as though he'd listened to everything she'd confided, but the meaning took a while to seep in. She was so downtrodden and forlorn, yet as soon as he did something that made her feel appreciated and needed, she came to life, her resilience almost shocking. Austin was neglecting the life out of her, the stupid asshole.

Asserting masculinity was a big game of king of the mountain and every guy wanted to be on top. Men, as a rule, were competitive beings, which was why Cord was in agreement with Austin. The greatest gift, the absolute victory of man, was in the graceful devotion of the woman he loved, wasn't it?

December was that sort of devoted woman, dedicating her energy to her home, a throne for her husband from which he could worship at her altar. She should have slapped him for trespassing on that.

Austin had a woman who was damn near perfect, indispensable in this day and age. They just didn't make 'em like that anymore. So why had she kissed him back?

Maybe because his friend let his kingdom collapse under months of insecurity, self-doubt, and alcohol abuse, and December was now changing as well. Cord greedily wanted the change, but rejected it all the same. Austin and December were right together. Anything else was wrong.

He just stole something priceless that belonged to his lost friend. What kind of self-serving prick preys on his friend's vulnerable wife? Shit. He was fucked up. The entire situation was fucked up. And then she'd gone and kissed him again—a small kiss, but still a kiss.

What did this mean?

He recalled the day Austin showed him the ring he planned to offer December, how happy and envious he was for his friend.

"Do you think she'll say yes?" Cord had asked, happy for his friend but sad to recognize this would permanently change a lot of things. Many of Cord's personal feelings would be overshadowed by Austin's true love—as it should be.

"I hope." It was the first time Austin seemed

the least bit nervous or unsure about anything, which spoke volumes about how much December meant to his friend.

Cord's mouth curved. There was no doubt in his mind December would agree to marry Austin. They were perfect together. Austin was an incredible man and December seemed like a great girl, really unique in the best ways. If he'd seen her first...

He shouldn't go there.

"I hope you know how lucky you are."

"I do." Austin nodded, his gaze fastened on the diamond cozied in the small velvet box. "I'm sorry."

"What?" Cord frowned, paranoia nipping at his gut. "What are you sorry for?"

Flashing that well-worn cocky grin, Austin knocked him with his shoulder and laughed. "Because there are plenty of women in the world, but I took the best one."

Cord laughed too, but with less humor. He should have realized Austin would sense his envy, even if he misread it. "She's a good girl, Austin. You're very lucky I let you get to her first."

And that was as close to the truth as he could go when he'd been working so hard to get over his feelings for...someone else when December walked into their lives. Maybe she was a godsend.

"You have no idea." Nothing would take that

grin off Austin's face. It was sort of sweet. "She takes my breath away. I don't deserve her."

"You're one of the best, Austin. If anyone deserves to be happy it's you."

His gaze turned serious. "Don't ever let me take her for granted, okay? I know I have faults, Cord. Don't let me get such a big head that I overlook the incredible gift she is, how lucky I am to have her even consider a life with me."

"I won't."

They were quiet for a while and then Austin asked the question Cord had been hoping to hear. "You'll be my best man, right?"

"Of course." It would be bittersweet, but he'd do it because no one else loved the two of them as fiercely as he. Not that anyone would ever know the true depth of it.

Austin chuckled. "Funny, our lives have always been so in sync, so tied together. I sort of imagined we'd find our soul mates at the same time. I hope one day you're as happy as I am now."

"Me too."

The door down the hall opened and Cord panicked. He'd been standing there rehashing the past the whole time she was in the bathroom.

Spinning around like he might conjure some magical escape hatch, he wasted precious seconds and came face to face with December *again*. Once more wrapped in a towel. Crap.

She appeared startled to find him still standing there, one hand lifting to her throat. Her skin was rosy from the shower and scrubbed clean. Damp hair hung down her naked back and over her shoulders. She blinked up at him questioningly.

"I'll go," he mumbled and quickly brushed past her. She smelled nice, like girl soap and cleanliness.

"Cord?"

He stilled at the end of the hall but didn't turn around. Déjà vu. God, he was an idiot. "Yeah?"

"Are we okay?"

He nodded. Sure. They were just dandy.

"Can you look at me?"

He shut his eyes and sighed. "I'd rather not right now, December. I'm sort of disappointed in myself."

"Please, look at me."

Reluctantly, he made a slow turn, but kept his eyes on the ground. She had such little feet with tinier toes. Shit. Those feet were stepping closer.

"Hey," she whispered, tugging on his shirt. "I don't want you to feel bad or awkward about what happened."

He met her gaze and smiled sadly. "I can't help it. Friends don't kiss their friend's wives."

"And good husbands don't drive their wives away, making them feel like a leper. I just have one question for you."

He waited for her to go on, only wanting to escape.

"Did you kiss me..." Regret flashed in her eyes. "Out of pity?"

"What? No!"

"Then why?"

"I don't know." His words rushed out of his mouth. "I just needed to, so I did, and now I'm sorry."

"Do you...feel...something for me?"

"I...Whatever I feel isn't relevant. Austin's always been like a brother to me. I've always put you in the role of little sister, but now..."

"Do you want me to stay somewhere else?"

No. Besides the fact she had nowhere else to go, a selfish part of him definitely wanted her to stay. "No."

"I'll go if you want me to. I'd understand."

Why did he have to fuck everything up when it was already a shit storm? A disapproving part of him was furious he'd made an awkward situation worse, but if she stayed he could prove his self-control. Right? Plus, she needed a friend and he wanted her to have one—and not have to worry about him taking advantage of her while she was in a vulnerable state. Jesus, he was a total douche.

"I want you to stay, December."

"I'm glad, because I don't want to go. But I need you to know that I love Austin. I love him more than what's probably healthy and once this is all over, and he straightens out his act, I'm going back to him. I love you, Cord. I don't regret the kiss, but..."

Ah, reality. What a cruel bitch. "I know. I never intended to interfere. I swear, I want you two to work this out. I never meant to add to your troubles. It was selfish and irresponsible of me and it *won't* happen again."

"Thank you."

He laughed, hoping she didn't hear the bitterness. "Why the hell are you thanking me?"

"Because, believe it or not, I desperately needed to be kissed."

And now he wanted to kiss her again. *Fuck my life.* "Goodnight, December."

"Goodnight, Cord."

He shuffled to his room, shutting the door and locking it behind him.

Fourteen

Cord

THE FOLLOWING morning he ran out to pick up conditioner, tissues and fancy creamer, something else he'd forgotten at the store. December was still sleeping, or at least she hadn't left her room. He hadn't slept more than a few hours and was up and dressed before dawn. On his way back to the house, he drove past her Jeep to make sure everything was okay.

"What the hell?" He pulled over to the side of the road when he noticed tracks and footprints surrounding the car in the newly fallen snow. He didn't have her keys with him and the doors were locked.

Pressing his face close to the frosted glass he frowned. Someone had been there. There was only one possibility, being that the backseat was filled with boxes and a note was taped to the steering wheel.

Worried at whatever this implied and how it would affect December, he returned to his truck and headed up the road to find—what he hoped would be—a sober Austin.

When he arrived at the house, the walk was shoveled and the truck was in a different place. He took the stairs quickly and knocked at the door before he entered. "Austin?"

"I'm in the kitchen."

Cord followed his voice and found him sitting at the table with a mug of what had better be coffee. "What the hell is all that stuff doing in December's car?"

Keeping his gaze on his mug, Austin said, "I fucked up."

"I know." His friend didn't look good.

"I know I don't deserve your forgiveness, but I'm sorry."

Cord moved farther into the room to lean against the counter. "I'm not the one you need to apologize to."

Austin shook his head. "I can't apologize to her."

"Why not?"

"She's heard it all before. Repeatedly. Empty bullshit."

"It's still nice to hear."

Austin breathed in a long breath and coughed it out. "I have a problem."

Yeah, he knew that too. "We want to help you, Austin."

Again his head shook. "I don't think you can. Well, that's not entirely true. You can, but not in the way you think."

"We just want you to be well, Austin. No one's given up on you."

"That's not the sort of help I'm looking for from you."

Cord frowned. "What are you talking about?"

"I need to quit drinking. For good. I've become a tyrant in my own home."

"Agreed."

There was a certain malevolence in Austin's glare, his eyes narrowing as a flush climbed his shadowed cheeks before it turned to resignation.

"It's so much harder than you could imagine. When I woke up, she was still gone. I was confused and sick. After I puked for about an hour, some things started coming back to me. How could I fucking treat her that way? I can't even imagine the parts I can't remember."

"Alcohol can be a vicious thing. First step to

recovery is recognizing there's a problem." That's how the saying went, right?

"*I'm* the problem. My head's not right."

Hearing a straight shooting man like Austin Garret admit such a thing broke his heart. "Whatever you need, you know I'll help you."

"There's so much pain. The ache in my chest, because I may have finally lost the love of my life, the regret and shame for how badly I've treated her, the loneliness of this unending isolation I've forced on myself. It's all killing me."

Cord's chest tightened as the urge to comfort his friend was restrained by his need to hear him finally admit the truth.

Keeping his gaze on the table, Austin went on. "Sometimes it hurts so bad I wonder if I drink to speed up the process and just get to the end. But I'm smarter than that. I know I am, and I know I have to stop. Then there's the withdrawal. You wouldn't think it could fuck a person up this bad but..." He held out a trembling hand. Cord didn't want to know how his other one got banged up. "I can't stop shaking and it's like my bones are shattering from the inside out."

"We're here for you." He hoped his reassurance would get through. "And there are people who can help you. Programs like AA..."

Austin, again, shook his head so Cord decided this was more a time to listen, since his friend was finally talking.

"I've done so much damage. My gut feels like it's been wrung out. I can't stop shivering. All I want to do is take a drink so the pain goes away, except I know I can't, because once I have one I can't stop. But nothing hurts more than knowing what I've put her through."

"We'll get you help. Therapy. Whatever it takes."

Back to avoiding his gaze, Austin remained focused on the mug in front of him, but his face twisted as if someone were stabbing him— slowly and repeatedly. In a broken whisper, he confessed, "Cord...I don't know if I hit her."

Cord's insides twisted. "I don't think so, but you scared her pretty good."

"The mirror in our room, the big one, it's shattered into a million pieces. There was blood on some of the shards."

"She cut her hand. Told me you kicked the mirror and broke it."

"God..." He gasped, but the explanation didn't seem to bring much relief as he bowed his head and silently sobbed. "Fuck... This isn't me. I'd never harm her. You know I wouldn't. I'd kill anyone that tried. I fucking love her."

Cord moved from the counter to crouch beside him, pressing a hand into his back. It was hard to say who his touch comforted more. "I know this isn't you, Austin. December knows too. That's why she's waiting for you to come back to her."

His shoulders shook under Cord's palm. "What if I can't? For the first time in my life I'm actually scared shitless I can't overcome this. I don't want her to be afraid of me, but how can I ask that of her when I'm terrified of myself?"

Cord was shit scared too. Every day this situation seemed bigger than the day before, more than anything they expected or were qualified to solve. And then there was his personal fuck up.

"You'll get help. You're one of the strongest people I know. You'll beat this."

Inhaling a deep breath through his nose, Austin drew his head up and wiped his mouth with the back of his hand, clearly schooling his emotions. "I need you to do something for me."

"Anything."

"She forgot some stuff she'll need. The book she was reading, those little hair ties she likes—the kind that don't pull—the rest of her clothes, and the lotion she rubs on her hands each night before bed. I put it all in her car."

He'd noticed and was worried by how much was actually there. "This isn't permanent, Austin. You'll enter a program, get your shit together, and she'll come back. She's just waiting for you to dry out and prove you're done drinking once and for all."

Knowing Austin all of his life made Cord well aware of his many expressions and how to translate them. When his friend leveled him with an utterly sobering stare, Cord's stomach bottomed out.

"No." There was that identifying Austin Garret resolve that they'd all been missing.

"What do you mean, *no*? Yes. You'll get help and fix your marriage."

"You don't understand. I've pushed her off for almost a year. It may take another year for me to get better. Maybe more. I want to be sober, but I can't promise I won't be drunk an hour after you leave."

"Then don't buy booze," he gritted, frustration pounding at his temples.

"I know!" Austin answered, sounding equally exasperated. "That's what I'm saying. It should be that simple, but it's not. Unless you're willing to put me on lockdown and babysit my ass, I can't promise I won't fuck up. I don't want that, not for you, not for her, and not for myself. I need to do this on my terms if I ever want to like myself again. I need to prove to myself I can beat this."

"What about what she wants? This is killing her, Austin."

"You have no idea how much I hate myself right now." A brittle, humorless laugh slipped past his lips. "Which only makes me want to drink even more."

"She'll wait for you. As long as it takes for you to get better, she'll wait."

"I don't want her to wait."

The blood pumping through Cord's veins solidified. Everything inside of him drew up tight as excoriating fear settled in. "What?"

"I don't want her to wait."

"I heard you the first time. What the hell does that mean?"

Austin gave him another hard stare. "It means her life shouldn't have to suffer one more minute longer than it already has for my mistakes. I want her to forget about me. At least for a while, until I can get my shit together. I want her to be happy."

"It doesn't work that way, man. You're her husband. She isn't happy unless you are."

"*You* make her happy. You can make her forget. You can distract her."

The hair on his neck rose as an ominous sensation grabbed hold and he took two staggering steps back. "I don't know what you're saying, but stop."

"No. This is what I want. I wrote her a letter and left it in her car. I want you to make sure she gets it. It explains everything. But before you do, I need you to promise me you're in."

"*In*? In what? You aren't making any sense."

"I want you to take care of her."

"I am—"

"More than that. I want you to be the husband I can't be right now."

He couldn't breathe. Taking another step back, he shook his head. "No."

Austin's eyes, so wrought with pain, shimmered. His cheekbones, no longer flushed with life resembled blades, slashed above his wooly beard. "She's so easy to love, Cord. It'll be...good for both of you. You'll finally have a good woman looking after you the way you deserve and she'll have someone to care for who's of sound mind, someone to appreciate her the way she deserves. She needs to be needed. You can need each other."

"It doesn't work that way, Austin. Jesus! Listen to what you're asking."

"You think I haven't thought this through?"

"No, I don't!" he snapped. "What you're suggesting is insane. It'll ruin everything!"

"The idea came in one of my rare moments of clarity, Cord. When I understood she could've been killed in that accident, when you rescued her. I hated you stepping in, but it stuck. You were there for her and I wasn't. I can't be, for

God knows how long. I know that whatever this is, it's bigger than me. Aside from her, I trust you most in this world. I trust you with the most important part of my sanity. I need you to guard her for me."

Anger, more than he'd felt through this entire mess, suddenly erupted inside of him. Yes, December was easy to love. A little too easy. Christ, he'd majorly fucked up last night when he kissed her. He couldn't do this. It was too risky.

And what the hell happened when Austin got his shit together? Where did that leave Cord? His friend was hedging his bets, asking too much of him. Cord would lose everything, because what Austin was suggesting was a whole galaxy away from normal. And December...she didn't want him. She wanted Austin. Why was he even vaguely entertaining this insanity?

"And what happens when this is all over and you're better? You come collect your estranged wife and I deal with the aftermath alone? You're asking me to love your wife so you can eventually take her back. This is real life, Austin, not layaway! What happens to our friendship? Mine with her and..." He could never agree to such a thing. "...and mine with you? What happens to us? To you two? You aren't thinking about the consequences, about what this will do to all of us in the end. She has feelings, goddamn it. *I* have fucking feelings!"

"*I need this from you!*" Austin roared. "Fuck the consequences! The consequences are now!" His breathing was shaky and loud. In a calmer voice, he begged, "*Please,* Cord. I need this from you."

He fucking begged, and Cord couldn't squeeze a breath in or out.

"Cord, I know what she needs and I can't give it to her. She needs intimacy, to be taken care of, needed. Guided. Just...love her. You'll see what she needs. Don't make me ask again."

"She'll hate you for this. She isn't an object you can pass around when you're feeling...tired, or incompetent or any such shit."

"Nor is she an object I can put on the shelf and ignore while I'm incapable of fulfilling the promises I've made. I swore she'd always be cared for, always get the love she needs. I gave her my word. It's my job to make sure she's valued and cherished—always. I need you to do this. It's *killing* me to let her go, but it's all I can do. My love for her is the only thing making that possible, no matter how much I know it'll destroy me to watch her go to another man. Even if that man is you."

Cord shut his eyes, dizzy with shock. "I can't do it. You're gambling too much."

"I've already put everything that means anything on the line. I've got nothing left to lose."

"You're wrong, Austin. You haven't lost her yet, but this will push her away more than anything else." *And wreck me, because I'll lose both of you.* "I'm sorry, but I can't be a part of what you're asking."

Austin laughed quietly. "You already are. I know you, Cord. Your actions speak louder than words. You've loved her as long as I have. You've just kept it under wraps. You don't have to hide your feelings anymore. I'm giving you my permission to…"

"I don't love her like that, and even if I did, I don't need your fucking permission," he snapped, tasting the bitter lie on his tongue. Austin didn't know the first thing about the feelings he hid. "She has a say, damn it, and I'm not interested. There are three people involved and regardless of your feelings—overlooking hers—I'm telling you, *I'm out.*" Even to his own ears his voice sounded unconvincing.

Reaching into his pocket, Austin pulled out the spare set of Jeep keys. "Don't let her come back here. I'll contact her when I'm ready. If she needs anything, *you* call me. I'll answer, but only for you. You need to protect her from me right now."

"Damn it, Austin—"

"Do this for me, Cord. It may be the kindest thing I ever do for you."

Or the cruelest. There was no reasoning with him. "Everyone will lose. This will only hurt people who've suffered enough."

"Then do it right, Cord. I know exactly what kind of man you are. Don't you dare rip her off by holding back, not on my account. I don't want her to suffer anymore."

Cord needed to make him see how terribly this could end for all of them, as in utter disaster. "Say I do it—"

"You will."

He gritted his teeth. "Shut up and listen. Say I do, who's to say I'll let her go when this is all over. You're playing with fire."

Austin smiled sadly. "My goal is to make her happy. If that's a life with you, someone I trust with her, then so be it."

"You don't mean that. I know you. You'd never truly let her go. You're asking me to violate something sacred. Don't do this, Austin."

His best friend gestured, weariness and re-solve mingling in the movement. "I'm gonna ask you to leave now. I've dumped all the liquor hidden around the house except for a few choice bottles. They're calling my name. I'm about to toast my beautiful wife and loyal friend and have my last hurrah. Hopefully, by the time I wake up, you'll have done the right thing and it'll be impossible to turn back. Trust me. Once you do, my opinion of you will be the least of your concerns. There's no loving her halfway, Cord. Just do what I ask so it can't be undone and it'll all fall into place from there. You're a good man. Remind her what that is, because I've made her forget and I don't know if I'll ever be good enough for her again."

"Austin..."

He had to make him reconsider. Cord had always loved her a little too much, though he'd locked those inconvenient feelings away for eons, buried deep with certain other feelings he refused to give voice to.

Everything was fine until Ember's proximity tinkered with those locks and now Austin was blowing the door off the hinges. Dangling this offer in front of him was too much temptation. Inconvenient feelings had to be juggled carefully and concealed. He was being torn in two.

"This isn't—"

"Get out of my house, Cord. I'm sober now and we both know I can kick your ass when I'm not swinging through a drunken fog. Knowing what you're about to do, it'll be no chore. Let's keep things civil for her sake. Sending you home with bruises will only make her hate me more."

"Damn it, Austin, she doesn't hate you!"

"She will once she reads my letter. Make sure she gets it." He reached under the table and produced a bottle. Unscrewing the metal cap, he tipped it over his mug. "Goodbye, old friend."

Speechless, accepting there was nothing else he could say to deter him, Cord backed his way out of the kitchen. Austin didn't spare him another glance, intent on his liquid poison.

He couldn't do it. There was no way. He'd give her the letter, but he wasn't taking his best friend's wife. Even if she would have him.

Fifteen

December

DECEMBER CRUMPLED the letter in her hands as a new level of agony ripped through her. How could he *do* this? She'd been crying since the first line.

I'm letting you go, because I love you.

She screamed through her teeth, "Motherfucking coward!"

Her hand shot out and she shoved all of her toiletries off the dresser and onto the floor. "*I hate you!* How could you do this to me?"

Strong arms wrapped around her, restraining her, and she fought them off. Her sobs tore through her, powered by a rage so tormented she could barely breathe or stand. When she crumpled to the floor Cord fell with her to the cold boards.

"Shh..." he soothed. It was no use. She'd never be the same again after reading that letter.

"How fucking dare he? I hate him," she whimpered, tremendous pain crushing her chest.

His arms banded around her and held her tight, slowly rocking. "No, you don't."

"Yes, I do. Did he tell you what *he* decided? Us? Me and you? Like we're fucking chess pieces? The fucking nerve! How does that solve anything?"

"It doesn't. I told him it wouldn't. It's a crazy idea. He isn't thinking clearly, Ember."

"Oh, he's thinking. He thinks he has it all figured out. I used to trust his judgment more than my own, but this... How could he suggest such a thing?"

Struggling free, she stumbled to sit on the bed, grabbing a pillow to clutch to her chest. Cord watched her, his face a mask of caution as she rocked. She had no idea what her expression conveyed, but she wanted to destroy everything. Shift into someone else.

Her fucking husband was giving her away... re-gifting her like a once favored possession that no longer held his interest. And to the man who'd helped them both. Was this Austin's way of punishing them? Because it most definitely guaranteed the ruin of their friendship.

"Ember, it'll be okay."

"I can't think. He's making me insane! I don't know what to do."

"Just breathe."

She squeezed the pillow tighter, her teeth grinding over a moan. "That son of a bitch. That *bastard!* He's truly lost his mind."

Screams welled up to release the wrath and humiliation burning inside her, and she buried her face in the pillow, muffling her cries as her sanity wavered. Scream after scream came out of her, impotent, but the pressure wouldn't ease. She pulled at her hair.

Cord's hands gripped her shoulders hard, as his sharp tone broke through her hysteria. *"Stop!"*

She stilled, their breathing the only sound in the quiet room.

The maelstrom of emotion iced over to frigid nothingness. Her face was soaked with tears as her mind hid some place she couldn't follow. It was all just...quiet.

"Stop," Cord whispered.

Numb, her body existed somewhere far away from her thoughts. Disoriented. She was there but at the same time she wasn't. The scattered pieces of her soul swept away on a bitter breeze, leaving nothing but a vacant cavity in her chest where her heart had once been.

Cord spoke soft words she couldn't decipher. She was far away. Lost. It was quiet and desolate. It was *her*, something was wrong with *her*.

Like a spinning wheel her body pulsed, as threads of her past wove into a tapestry she could no longer recognize. Tattered edges were cut away and discarded, too untidy to keep, too imperfect to salvage. He'd tossed her out like those scraps, thrown to the wind, certain that someone else would collect the pieces. Not just someone. His best friend.

Her face pressed into the pillow as the weight of Cord's hand remained her only anchor to this world.

Shutting her eyes, she shivered, a chill cutting through the delirium that was her broken mind. So silent. So cold. Alone again. Her thoughts danced and stilled, drifting off on clouds of hope too far for her to reach. Slowly, her mind let go and the quiet became a numbing comfort.

When her eyes again opened her heart was calm and her tears had dried. A cocoon of distant numbness tucked protectively around her. She sought the clock on the nightstand. Had she slept? Cord was gone. Her mind struggled to focus.

Austin.

Darkness filled her. She couldn't conjure his face no matter how hard she tried.

Austin.

Perhaps her rage had destroyed her memories.

Slipping out of bed, she wandered through the silent house that was not her own and found herself in the bathroom. She stood, staring at the mirror for a long time.

He was punishing her when all she'd been was a good wife. Giving her away butchered those last tender pieces of her heart.

Anger surged. Worthlessness, and a sense of rejection, ate at her belly like maggots. Not a vengeful person, yet the urge to retaliate took root and blossomed.

She stood for an eternity, the woman in the mirror so unfamiliar, a stranger she used to know. The solution would present itself, the bad dream would end, and everything would fall into place. She merely had to stand there a little longer.

No matter how long she stood, starring at her lost reflection, no answers came. She had a job, and a debt to pay. She couldn't take time off for yet another breakdown in her decaying life.

She bathed without thought, dressing and pulling back her hair with rote motions. When she entered the kitchen, Cord surveyed her from where he stood at the stove, his presence a familiar one she was quickly growing accustomed to in her life.

A hint of need for comfort tempted her, too easy to embrace, too terrifying to face. Cord had become as dependable as Austin once was, yet he wasn't Austin at all. Maybe she liked that about him.

"Morning," he greeted, voice as steady as a mountain.

She was eternally glad he didn't ask how she was. She didn't know. "Morning."

"I made eggs. And coffee."

Nodding her appreciation, she grabbed two plates from the cupboard and some utensils from the drawer beneath. Cord poured coffee, and she doctored hers, finding a modicum of strength in the simplest of routines. The liquid swirled into the dark brew and she stared, mesmerized at the sight. Her thoughts were swirling much the same, into the deep.

"Ember?"

Pulling her attention back, she forced a smile, feeling the corners of her lips stretch uncomfortably. Cord smiled in return, but it looked as hollow as hers felt.

"You don't have to go in today."

"I'm good." She took a swallow of coffee, wishing it would warm her icy insides.

He served her a helping of eggs, and put some on his plate. "If you want to talk—"

"I'm done talking, Cord. I'm thinking." Sweet of him to offer, but there was nothing left to say.

He winced.

"I can't get my head around anything right now, anyway," she said, by way of apology.

Opening his mouth, he shut it again, and they concentrated on the food.

He warmed the truck and shoveled the walk while she cleared the table and sorted the dishes —the hint of normalcy a tiny balm. They drove in silence, an uncomfortable one that Cord filled by incessantly turning the dial of the radio, but she didn't mind. She tried to drum up some energy, hoping the busy hours ahead would offer a distraction.

The moment they entered the store, Cord

mumbled a polite excuse and quickly made his escape to the back while she fell into position behind the register. Her apron fit like a bullet-proof vest, protecting her from the domestic failures lurking outside those glass doors.

Working doggedly through the day, she felt disconnected...from the customers, from the job itself, from life in general. Cord hovered for long moments at a time, his face betraying his worry and concern.

When several minutes passed without even a sigh passing her lips, he'd slip away, disappearing on some errand in the far regions of the empty store. Despite it being a rather slow day, it seemed she hadn't earned a second of rest. The emptiness was crippling, yet her mind whirled. She needed...

"Time to close, Ember. Long day. We'll pick up Chinese for dinner. Save us cooking."

He was so good to her, patient and tolerant of her silence when she'd run out of things to say, seeking to make her life easier by ordering in.

She helped him with the closing routine and made an effort to respond to his small talk on the drive home. The takeout's fragrant scent permeated the vehicle, the heat of the boxes bringing a good burn to her lap, one she hoped might thaw the frigid ice still creeping through her veins.

Maybe she should have insisted that she cook

for him. Where was her place in life? Where were the boundaries? The expectations? She was just... floating. Lost.

As delightful as the scent of ribs and fried rice was, the sight only twisted her empty stomach another degree. Unable to eat, she pleaded exhaustion and retreated to her room—or the room she'd been assigned during this displaced chapter of her life. Cord's anxiety reverberated through the walls of the house, following her as she huddled beneath the covers.

Just a little while longer, until she figured out what she needed. Sooner or later a page would turn.

Sixteen

Cord

CORD WOKE to the sound of someone entering his room and shifted to sit up, his vision straining through the dark. "December?"

His eyes adjusted to the shadows as her silhouette passed through the pale moonlight streaking from the window. Blinking his way out of sleep, he wondered if he was still dreaming. Glancing at the clock on the night table, he saw it was nearly dawn.

He'd watched over her all day, reluctantly leaving her alone with her thoughts, always waiting for her to break, but she never did—not since her response to reading that horrible letter.

Leaving her be hadn't felt like the right choice, but he needed the distance from her and the temptation assaulting him from every angle. He couldn't think around her, or force Austin's proposal out of his head.

"Are you okay?"

She didn't answer. The mattress dipped as she climbed into his bed.

"Ember?"

The silence cranked up his heart rate. Her heated body slipped closer and the breath jerked sharply into his lungs as her hand touched his shoulder.

Jesus Christ, she wasn't wearing a shirt. No bedding separated her lush curves from his rapidly hardening body. He sucked in another breath as her arm settled over his bare chest and her breasts pressed against him, abruptly awakening all his senses. This had to be a dream.

"December, what are you doing?" He shuffled back as much as he could in the tangled sheets.

"Exactly what he asked."

Fuck! He scrambled out from under the covers and flipped on the lamp. Shit, she was completely naked! He looked away. "I think you should go back to your room. Now."

Silence.

His stomach pinched with uncertainty.

Crap, she'd gone through hell, thought Austin had rejected her, and *he* didn't want to hurt her feelings, but they *could not* do this.

"In his letter...he said you've always...cared about me, wanted me. Is that true, Cord?"

His throat was dry as sand, constricting painfully as he attempted to swallow.

Goddamn you, Austin.

With tense, shifting movements, he made himself look at her, but couldn't make himself talk. Mouth tight, he begged her with his eyes. *Don't do this...*

Rising to her knees, pulling the sheet against her chest, her features twisted with what looked to be shame, mingled with brutal determination. But not...love.

"Cord?"

Squeezing his eyes shut, he forced the words out. "You need to go back to your own bed, December. You're upset and this isn't what you want."

Her head lowered, her expression flashing utter dejection and humiliation before a curtain of chocolate waves hid her face. "I won't let him choose for me. I've thought long and hard about this, Cord, and it's my choice, not his."

"You're upset," he repeated, knowing she was in no state of mind to make such a decision.

"Yes, I'm upset. I'll likely be upset for a long

time being that the man I trusted above all else threw me away. But I also trust you. I'm not worthless and I refuse to go where I'm unwanted. If you truly want me to go, I will. But if there was any truth to his accusations and you want me... I'd be lying if I said part of me didn't want you too. I haven't forgotten our kiss."

Fuck. He kept his eyes trained on the wall as the bedding rustled. Frantic to find the right solution to this mess, he spoke quickly. "Austin wasn't thinking clearly when he wrote that letter, December. We're friends. *All* of us. Doing what he asked would ruin everything."

"I know this isn't what you asked for, but right now, I feel...dead inside." Her confession came out so jagged it no longer became a fight to prove Austin wrong, but a battle to keep his distance and somehow comfort her, the woman he cared deeply about when she was laying herself bare in every sense of the word.

"Ember, I do love you, but..."

"I'm scared. I've never been so afraid or felt so unwanted. I just... Could you just take away my fear for a few minutes so the last of me doesn't shatter?"

Jesus. Pain tightened around his heart as he sympathized with her desperate plea and dredged up the courage to face her. That was a mistake.

Her small breasts were full and perfect, tipping upward with the sweetest little pink nipples. Her belly was soft and ultra-feminine. Her pussy was shaved and by the way she sat on her knees, surrounded by his rumpled covers, he could see a bit of pink peeking from her slit.

His body hardened to granite under his sweats. No way could she miss his arousal. Fuck Austin. Fuck him and his stupid letter and his goddamn selfish fucking demands. Fuck his *own* desperate need. Fuck everything, because deep down he desperately wanted to fuck her. And it wasn't only that. He wanted to *have* her, not part of her or her affection on loan, but all of her. His dominant streak demanded it. And that was impossible.

They'd all wind up getting hurt, but in the end, Cord had no doubt Austin would conquer his demons. December would go back to him, and their friendship would be strained, awkward, *over*. Irretrievable, like a snapshot in time none of them would ever find again, leaving him, more than anyone else, alone, aching for something he never deserved in the first place, but he was too weak to refuse. And too damn courteous to ask for such a chance ever again.

Shallow breaths tightened his lungs. She was stunning. She was everything he ever wanted, but would never truly have. He shut his eyes.

She'll never be yours. She'll always be his and

he'll always be hers and you'll wind up losing them both.

"I can't," he wheezed.

He couldn't do this. He couldn't have her then give her back. Austin couldn't expect such a sacrifice, not when he suspected Cord's hidden feelings for her all these years—not to mention the other feelings Cord hoped were still safe from anyone's perusal. There was simply too much at stake. There'd be nothing left of him when it was over. He'd rather not know what he'd been missing.

Her gaze lowered and she looked so devastated he hated himself for adding to her misery. She slowly stood without making eye contact and walked to the door.

Her hair fell to her hips in a perfect drape of chestnut and her sweet ass... His hands trembled so fiercely he drew them into fists, his knuckles cracking in the silence.

Everything inside of him, aside from his dwindling honor, wanted to call her back, but he couldn't. He deserved a partner who actually chose him *first*. He was no man's proxy.

Wordlessly, she left the room and he exhaled some of the pent up frustration and self-restraint. Twisting, he gritted his teeth and cut his reach short before he punched the wall. He wasn't like Austin in that way.

Then he heard it.

A single gut-wrenching sob, destroying the last of his noble resolve.

"Fuck."

There would be no pity in this should his honor buckle. Laying the slightest hand on her would betray the secrets he guarded all these years, because once he touched her she'd know without a doubt how deeply he truly cared, how freaking hard he'd struggled with letting the best man—and woman—win. But where was that man now?

Enough thinking.

He charged from his room and caught up with her, stepping against her back. She let out a startled cry as he caught her full hips in his hands, spinning her in the dark hallway. She gasped and he pressed her back to the wall.

"I'm sorry," he muttered as his mouth closed over hers, his senses reveling as though it was the first rain after a decade of droughts.

He lifted her by her soft ass and her arms wreathed tightly around his neck as her breasts pressed into his chest. Goddamn, she felt perfect up against him, flesh to flesh. Pinning her harder against the wall, he kissed her with every ounce of desire he'd been denying since the day they met.

"I fucking want you, Ember," he rasped,

dragging his lips from her mouth to her jaw. "I don't need to pretend a love that's been there all along."

Her legs tightened around his hips as he hitched her pliant body higher, supporting her soft behind in his palms. His cock eagerly pressed against the fabric of his pants, reaching for her core, but first things first.

He bit at the tiny lobe of her ear and she moaned. Sucking hard, he released it with a groan. His breath beat against the side of her fluttering pulse as he licked, nibbled, and whispered, "I want you to listen to me, Ember. If we do this, you accept that it's *me* you're with. I will not be a substitute for him. You either want me —*me*—or you don't, but I need to know right fucking now. I don't have room in my life for make believe."

"I want you," she breathed.

"Say my name."

"Cord." The word fanned hot over his shoulder, breathing fire into his veins.

His mouth sucked on her flesh, eager to mark her. "Say it again."

"Cord." She breathed it out, caressing him with her voice.

His cock swelled painfully. "Do you want me, December?"

"Yes. Please."

"There's no undoing this."

Her limbs tightened, squeezing him deliciously. "I know what I want, Cord. I want you. Please. Don't make me beg anymore."

He carried her back to his room, a precious bundle huddled close. Following her plush body down to the mattress, his mouth trapped hers in a searing kiss, keeping her present. Her petite form shifted beneath him as if the sensation was already too much to bear.

Her folds, wet with arousal, pressed against his belly. He slid his hand over the soft curve of her belly and between her warm thighs. "Look at me, Ember."

Her feathery lashes lifted and she stared at him, her pupils dilated, the brown irises reflecting the shaded dawn.

"Is this what you want?" The tip of his finger tickled the protruding nub of her clit.

She arched into him. "Yes."

"You need my fingers inside of you?"

"Yes, Cord, please."

"Then ask for it." This was between him and her, by God, only him and her.

Intimacy shattered every wall he'd built between them as she stared into his eyes. "Please, Cord... Put your fingers inside of me."

His dick twitched at her plea. Sliding two fingers between her folds, he penetrated deep, and she pressed into his touch, her tight channel a narrow fit. Reality flickered in and out of the surreal moment, throwing off his usual confidence, but her moan urged him on. He worked his digits relentlessly, feathering his thumb over her clit.

"Eyes on me."

She blinked and her gaze connected with his, bonding with him on more than a physical level. Like a thirsting woman in a desert, he saw the moment she trusted her needs would be quenched—the moment she truly saw *him*.

A delicate gasp of anticipation preceded the arch of her spine. Her fingers tightened at his side, nails digging delectably into his flesh. "God, Cord, don't stop."

He'd give her everything she needed, everything she'd been starved of. Sucking one sharp nipple into his mouth, he relished the way her pussy rippled around his fingers. He gently bit the tender tip and another gasp filled the room, a rush of satisfaction hitting him hard.

"Beautiful," he muttered, against her distended flesh.

Her ass lifted as she rode his hand, chasing an orgasm. When he withdrew his fingers she whimpered in protest.

"Shh."

Her hands clutched at the sheets, but she

stilled at his command. So compliant. So exquisite. Everything he wanted in a woman.

He soothed her with the gentle tracing of his lips between her breasts, then peppered tiny kisses over her fragrant skin as he traveled down her body. Kneeling at the foot of the bed, he grasped her calves, tugged her closer, and pushed her knees wide.

Her pinkest flesh unveiled and he groaned at the sight. Her unique scent drew him closer, and he leaned in to lap at the cream coating her folds.

His eyes rolled back in pleasure at the first true hint of her. "You taste amazing."

She moaned as he drew back, her breathing shallow and choppy. "I need…"

"I know, sweetheart. But I want to take my time." Tracing her soft, rosy perfection elicited sweet whimpers. "My God, you're flawless."

His wrist turned as he slowly sank his fingers deep. Her arousal drenched his skin, the pearl of her clit prominent at her apex. His mouth closed over it and suckled with the rhythm of his fingers.

"Oh my God. Oh my God! *Oh my God!*" Her pussy tightened like a vise around his fingers and he pumped hard as she came—too soon and not nearly enough to satisfy either of them.

"Another," he commanded, blowing cool air over her clit and teasing her with the tip of his tongue. He advanced past her swollen tissue, stretching her. Sultry heat flowed around his digits as one orgasm rolled into another.

She writhed, nails scratching against fabric, her belly and thighs glistening with sweat. Gliding the palm of his other hand above her mound, he pinned her flat. "Feel me, Ember. Me."

When he crooked his fingers toward the front of her channel, grazing his thumb at her mound just over her clit, she shattered. "Cord!"

His nostrils flared at the affirmation that she was right there with him, aware that it was *his* touch bringing her such pleasure. That she wanted *him*. Strong muscles rippled and convulsed beneath his splayed palm. It was time. He couldn't deny himself another moment.

Reaching into his nightstand, he fumbled for a condom and tore it open. Her scent was everywhere, on his fingers, his lips, in the air. It was an intoxicating opiate he couldn't get enough of.

Shoving away his pants, he sheathed his anxious cock, then positioned Ember in the center of the bed. She lay splayed beneath him and he took a moment to simply appreciate her unparalleled beauty.

I love her. I love them.

Not ready to face tricked truths, he couldn't

help but fall into her chocolate gaze. He wasn't giving her back. Ever.

Pressing his engorged cock to her sex, her body welcomed him home. Air sucked into his lungs as he throbbed deep inside of her. Pure ecstasy licked up his spine as he sighed, "December."

Her lush lips formed a gentle smile as her gaze softened. "Cord."

The need for proclamations of love rushed through his mind, but he held them back. He'd earn her love, wouldn't extract it from a sense of obligation or desperation or, god forbid, gratitude.

Slowly thrusting forward, every stroke of her tight passage was heaven. Her hands reached out, fingers ghosting over his lips and cheeks. Though he'd had sex countless times in his life, no one had ever touched or watched him so intimately.

Her fingers were so soft, her touch so delicate. She never took her eyes off of him. When her caress worked through his hair, a guttural groan escaped from low in his throat.

"I've always loved your curls," she whispered.

He rotated his hips, taking his time. The age-old dance of making love suddenly seemed new and fresh. "We're going to talk about all the things I love about you, sweetheart. That I've always loved." He might be admitting too much, but there was no holding back now.

"Kiss me, Cord. I need to feel your lips on mine."

Taking her mouth possessively he tangled his tongue with hers. His cock pulsed as his thrusts faltered, staving off his orgasm. He never wanted this closeness to end, but the sensations were too powerful to deny.

He came in a rush of heat as Ember shuddered in yet another climax. Euphoria surged from the depths of his soul, bleaching every dark shadow out of his vision in a blaze of white ecstasy unlike anything he'd ever experienced before.

Austin's face flashed in his mind.

Ghostly fingers chilled his spine as incomprehensible guilt rained down on him, unleashing a storm of shame and washing away the momentous pleasure in a flood of reality that came with a skewed sense of privilege and regret. Fuck. He pressed his face to her shoulder and caught his breath.

What had they done?

Seventeen

Austin

SOMETHING YANKED Austin out of a dead sleep. His chest tightened unbearably as if a ton of bricks were crushing him. *Am I having a heart attack?*

Falling off the couch, he gripped his chest. Sweat broke out over his entire body as he forced his faltering lungs to draw in air.

I can't breathe. I can't fucking breathe!

Pressing his shoulder into the carpet he tried to calm the anxiety racing through him. Something was terribly wrong.

Gasping for air, he wheezed, "December."

The pain receded as he conjured her face in

his mind, but the panic remained. What had he done? Rolling to his back he moaned, shutting his eyes and praying for the claustrophobic feeling to recede.

His head throbbed as he choked, still trying to regulate his breathing. He squinted toward the window. Tears pricked his eyes as his cracking heart accepted his edict had come to pass.

It was done. He knew it. Some cosmic power communicated that his marriage was over at his orders. The pain of such a realization resonated through him like cannon fire.

"Fuuuuuck," he bellowed through his teeth as he breathed harshly, the sharp pain in his chest stabbing harder than before.

Calm down. Calm down. Breathe. Calm. Calm.

The longer the pain carried on, the more convinced he became that he was going to die. He couldn't die. He had to fix things with December—or at least make sure she was happy again before he left this fucked up world. He had to do right by her. He couldn't allow her last memory of him be one of fear and failure.

His vision blurred and he rolled to his side, certain he was about to be sick. Dry heaving and sweating, he forced out her name over and over again, clinging to it like a lifeline.

"Ember." He shut his eyes, imagining her sweet smile.

"Ember." The scent of her hair.

"December." The sound of her laugh.

His breathing slowed, but pressure still constricted his chest, too much to draw a full breath. Somehow he managed shallow ones.

"December Skye." Her name gave his breathing a pace to follow. Inhale her first name, exhale her middle. "December...Skye."

As time passed and the episode faded, his thoughts wandered. Tears slipped from his eyes but, for once, there was no shame in crying. It was the greatest agony he'd ever know—losing her.

Such a good girl, she'd done just as he'd asked. Letting her go to a better man was the only thing he could do to protect her. He'd fucked up, pure and simple, betrayed her and abused her. December, his precious wife.

If he couldn't get better, he had to make her stop loving him. She needed to let him go so she could believe in someone worthwhile again. Cord would never let her down.

And if, by some miracle, Austin pulled himself back on track, he'd spend his life winning her heart all over again, but for now, this was how it had to be. It was his last effort at loving her—letting her go.

However long it took, he'd do what he had to do and somehow keep breathing—for her.

TO BE CONTINUED...

The story is far from over!
Read BANG (Addicted to You 2) Now!

Are you follow Lydia Michaels?
Stalk her on <u>TikTok</u>, <u>Instagram</u>, <u>Facebook</u>, <u>Goodreads</u>, and <u>BookBub</u>!
<u>TikTok @LydiaMichaels</u>
<u>Instagram @lydia_michaels_books</u>
<u>Facebook @LydiaMichaels</u>
<u>Goodreads</u>
<u>BookBub</u>

Also by Lydia Michaels

BOOKS BY SERIES

Many first in series books are FREE

Grab them here!

Free Books Here!

MCCULLOUGH MOUNTAIN

Almost Priest *

Beautiful Distraction

Irish Rogue

British Professor

Broken Man

Controlled Chaos

Hard Fix

Intentional Risk

JASPER FALLS
Wake My Heart *
The Best Man
Love Me Nots
Pining For You
My Funny Valentine
Side Squeeze

CALAMITY RAYNE
Calamity Rayne Gets a Life *
Calamity Rayne Back Again
Calamity Rayne Gets Hitched
BONUS: Calamity Rayne Veiled & Railed
Calamity Rayne Over the Moon
Calamity Rayne Knocked Up

THE SURRENDER TRILOGY
Falling In
BreakingOut
Coming Home

Ruthless Billionaires

One Billion Secrets *

Two Billion Enemies

MASTERMIND

Blind

Untied

NEW CASTLE

First Comes Love *

If I Fall

Shattered Vows

ADDICTED TO YOU

Crush *

Bang

Throb

THE ORDER OF VAMPIRES

Original Sin *

Dark Exodus

Prodigal Son

Immortal Bastard

Primal Kill

Blood Moon

STAND ALONES

La Vie en Rose

Simple Man

Sugar

Breaking Perfect

Hurt

Protege

About the Author

To receive Lydia's Newsletter and 7 FREE Books, click HERE !

Free Books Here!

Lydia Michaels is the bestselling and award-winning author of more than forty novels. She writes heart-clenching, unpredictable romance with dark elements and high heat. Her work is character-driven and bursting with broken heroes and badass females. With a sweet spot for overbearing, territorial types, her deeply emotional books are spicy, emotionally satisfying, and guaranteed to leave readers with many book hangovers.

Lydia is the consecutive winner of the *2018 & 2019 Author of the Year Award* from *Happenings Media* and the recipient of the *2014 Best Author Award* from the Courier Times. She has been featured by *USA Today*, *Romantic Times Magazine*, the *Women in Publishing Summit*, and more.

Michaels started her author career in 2007, becoming a recognized presence and advocate within the publishing industry. She is the CEO of LMC Consulting, a certified author coach specializing in character and plot development, and the founder of the *East Coast Author Convention*, the *Behind the Keys Author Retreat*, and <u>www.LydiaMichaelsBooks.com</u>.

She is happily married to her childhood sweetheart. Her favorite things include cooking Italian cuisine, hosting extravagant dinner parties, sipping espresso martinis, listening to her husband play piano, and escaping to her coastal home on the Jersey Shore. She's an LGBTQ ally, a BLM supporter, a firm believer that the patriarchy must end (women's rights are human rights), and an advocate for pediatric cancer research.

Follow Lydia Michaels on social media!
Facebook | Instagram | TikTok

Thank you for your review!

Reviews help authors so much! If you left a review for this book, I greatly appreciate it!
Thank you,
Lydia

Click here to leave your review!

Acknowledgement

This trilogy haunted me. I started it during a very difficult time in my life and wasn't sure I had the courage to write it to the end. At the time, I struggled to finish anything. But certain people encouraged me not to give up and, because of them, I picked myself up and carried on. I hope you have people in your life like that, too.

Every character in this story is beautifully human, understandably flawed, and perfectly imperfect. We all face challenges but sometimes lack the courage to fully heal or the belief that happiness is possible when there is also unwelcomed change.

The last mile of any journey is always the hardest, and sometimes we need a good friend to walk those final steps by our side. For me, that person was Trudy.

This story was almost finished but far from done. It was a pebble in my shoe that I felt every day in every shaky step I took toward an uncertain end. I wasn't sure if I'd ever finish it, if I'd ever write again, but Trudy helped me find my way.

Sometimes, the challenges we face are so overwhelming we can't see a way past them, but outsiders see into the storm and pull us through. Between the lines of this love story, you can feel the storm closing in, but I promise sunshine waits on the other side.

I owe so much of this series success and my own to Trudy. She was among the first to recognize my talent as a writer and encouraged me from the start. She picked me up when I was down and held my hand when I struggled to go on. This story, and many others, might not have made it to you without her unflagging support behind the scenes. And that is exactly what this trilogy is about, the unconditional love and support of friends when we need them most.

Trudy was so much more than an executive

developmental editor on this project. She was a mother, a friend, a collaborator, a therapist, a teacher, a realist, an optimist, and a constant source of encouragement and hope. She helped me get that pebble out of my shoe so I could move on. She helped me more than she will probably ever realize.